I0778397

Guy Thorne

The Hypocrite

Outlook

Guy Thorne

The Hypocrite

1. Auflage | ISBN: 978-3-73263-086-8

Erscheinungsort: Frankfurt am Main, Deutschland

Erscheinungsjahr: 2018

Outlook Verlag GmbH, Frankfurt.

Reproduction of the original.

THE HYPOCRITE

A FEW

EARLY PRESS OPINIONS

OF

THE HYPOCRITE

MORNING POST:—"It is entitled to be regarded as one of the clever books of the day."

MORNING LEADER:—"A brilliant book…. Evidently the work of a young, powerful, and subtle brain."

WORLD:—"The anonymous author is evidently young and clever. He paints with a firm, bold hand. The characters are life-like, and in many cases drawn from the life. The book will be found interesting and entertaining."

LONDON MORNING:—"A remarkable book…. Clever the book undoubtedly is. Its brutally frank analysis of the temperament of a man with brain and mind hopelessly diseased lifts the author out of the common rut of novelists, and stamps him as a writer of power."

LLOYD'S:—"The book sparkles with epigrammatic sayings and satirical allusions. The characters are all vividly drawn, some of them being undoubted and recognisable caricatures. The writing is that of a clever pessimist, with a vein of sardonic humour that keeps the reader amused. The author may wear a green carnation, but whether he does or not, it is the work of a skilful pen."

THE HYPOCRITE

LONDON

GREENING & CO.

1898

SECOND IMPRESSION

First Edition   November, 1898
Reprinted   December, 1898

THE HYPOCRITE

CHAPTER I.

YARDLY GOBION OPENS HIS LETTERS.

"I am thinking of writing my impressions, binding them in red leather, with a *fleur-de-lys* stamped in the corner, and distributing them among my friends," said the youth with the large tie.

"My good fool," said the President of the Union, who sat by the fire, "you must remember that most of us know you are a humbug."

"Quite so, but I'm not going to do it for the journalistic set. Don't you know that, owing to my youthful appearance and earnest eyes, I have an admiring circle of people who worship me as their god—good, healthy, red people, who like moonlight in the quad, and read leading articles? It is very amusing. I wear a great mass of hair, and look at them with far-away eyes instinct with intellectual pain; and sometimes when we get very solemn, the tears rise slowly, and I talk in clear tones of effort, of will—the toil, the struggle, the Glorious Reward! They absolutely love me, and I live on them, borrow their allowances, drink their whiskey—in short, rook them largely allround."

"It is a good thing," said a Merton man, whom they called the Prophet, "that you have an ark of refuge, where there is no necessity to pose, and where you can freely behave like the scoundrel you are; soul-scraping with earnest freshmen is doubtless profitable, but I should say it was wearing."

"That's the worst of it. I have to disguise the fact that I know you people, and write for *The Dead Bird*; it is horribly difficult. I find, though, that when I am just a little drunk I do it much better. One can look more *spirituel*, and play the game better all round. Unfortunately the entrances and exits require management. When one is leaning back in a padded armchair, it is easy to appear sober; but coming into a big room full of men, and picking one's way through them to get to the aforesaid chair, is very perilous work."

"'Where there's a swill there's a sway,' I suppose," said the Prophet.

"Exactly," said the youth, with a yawn; "you are becoming singularly apt at a certain sort of machine-made epigram. I will have a short drink—quite short. Yes, please—Scotch——" He splashed some soda-water into his tumbler from a syphon on the table, drank it off at a gulp, and got up.

"I really must go now; I am to speak third at the Wadham debate, so I mustn't be late."

He got his hat—a soft felt one—and arranging his tie in the glass over the mantelpiece, went out with a smile. The rooms belonged to the President of the Union, who was living out of college. They were rooms arranged with an eye to effect; the owner posed in his furniture as well as in his person, though there was no particular evidence of luxury or straining after cheap æstheticism.

A few armchairs, a sideboard covered with bottles, and two large bookshelves full of paper-backed novels of Heller and Maupassant, with a few portly historical treatises of the Taswell-Langmead type, were the most prominent objects.

It was evident, however, that a central idea influenced the arrangement. Sturtevant wrote little decadent studies for any London paper that would take them. He had scattered notes from literary people about the mantelpiece. The table was covered with proof-slips, magazines, and empty glasses, while his latest piece of work, a thin book bound in brown paper, called *The Harmonies of Sin*, lay in a conspicuous place on the window-seat.

When Yardly Gobion, the youth who had been speaking, had gone, Sturtevant and the Prophet, whose real name was Condamine, drew up their chairs to the fire, lighting fresh cigarettes. They had been drinking all day, and were by this time in the stage that knows no reticence. It is the stage immediately preceding a pious fervour and resolve to start a new life.

Both of them were men of mark in the University.

Sturtevant had come up to Oxford with a brilliant scholarship from a public school which was growing in reputation every year, the Head-master being a high churchman who made a scientific study of advertising his own personality in the weekly press as an earnest ascetic, but who in reality was merely a Sybarite masquerading as a monk. Sturtevant was the show boy of Hailton, and soon made himself felt in his year at Oxford.

He spoke well and brilliantly at the Union and various college debating societies. He affected an utter disregard for morals, pretending so vigorously that Irish whiskey was entirely necessary to salvation that he soon came to believe in his own pose, and to find a day impossible without frequent "short drinks."

Though his eyesight was excellent he carried a single eyeglass, and on alternate days wore a hunting stock or a Liberty yellow silk tie.

The extraordinary thing about the man was that he was not merely a poseur; he really had remarkable cleverness, and despite his life he had done excellently well in the Schools and Union. In this his last term he was at the head of things literary, and of the "Modern" school at Oxford.

Condamine was a different type of man. He had done nothing very much but talk, but had a great influence with the cleverest set. He was tall, with a white, clean-shaven face, and an oracular way of holding forth which had earned him the name of Prophet. He lived as if life were a painful duty which he must perform, but very much against his inclination.

He was a very high churchman, who on Sunday mornings might often be seen walking up the aisle of St. Barnabas carrying a richly-illuminated mass-book. "Sunday," he would say, "should be a day of rest." He defined himself as a psychological hedonist.

"Young Gobion is a very clever blackguard," said the Prophet.

"Yes, he is," said Sturtevant; "he looks so young and innocent, and he talks well."

"Is he a pure adventurer?"

"No, I don't quite think that; he comes of a good family, but they won't have anything to do with him, and for the last term or two he has been living on his wits. He's nearly done now, though. I should think he'd drop out after this term."

"I never knew how far to believe the man. I suppose he does write a good deal?"

"Yes, that's quite true. I've seen his things in *The Book Review* and in *The Pilgrim*. I imagine too he makes a good deal out of the Church party."

"What on earth do you mean?"

"Why, he acts a fit of remorse and horror at the life he is leading, goes to Father Gray to confession, and then borrows ten pounds to start a new life."

Sturtevant laughed an evil little snigger and poured out some more whiskey.

They had blown out the lamp as the oil was low, and the room was only lighted by the dull glow of the dying fire. The air was heavy with cigarette smoke and the smell of spirits, and both men felt bored and sleepy.

Condamine was afraid a fit of depression was approaching, so he raised himself in his chair, and began to drive away his thoughts by telling Sturtevant risky stories.

They were far too clever to really care much for cheap nastiness, but both felt it a relief from the state of nervous tension that a long day's continuous drinking had induced.

"One touch of indecency makes the whole world grin, to paraphrase the immortal bard," he said, and they both laughed and sighed.

Suddenly a man in the rooms above who had a piano began to play the Venusberg music from *Tannhäuser* very quietly.

Almost simultaneously with the beginning of the music the moon, like a piece of carved silver floating through the winter sky, attended by a little drift of fluffy amber and sulphur-coloured clouds, swung round from behind New College tower, sending a broad band of green light across the room.

Sturtevant's white face was thrown into sharp relief against the shadow.

Condamine sat quite still, shivering a little. He felt cold. The strange music tinkled on, like the overture to some strange experience, sounding almost unearthly to those two unhappy souls in the room below.

Sturtevant's face twitched. His nerves were all wrong, and he was subject to small facial contortions.

The moon moved farther away from the tower, and, peeping over a gargoyle, shone still more directly into the room. On the wall opposite the window was a picture of the Dutch realistic school, a heavy hairless face, fat, with a look of vacuous excitement.

Condamine stared fixedly at it.

Suddenly the music stopped, and the man above shut the piano with a bang that jarred among the strings.

Condamine jumped up with a curse, looking as if he had been asleep. Then he yawned, and taking his cap and gown, without speaking left the room.

It was then upon nine o'clock, and he went to the Union and fought depression by firing off epigrams to a crowd of men in the smoking-room with the assured air of a man of vogue.

The Wadham debate was over about eleven, and soon after the hour had struck, Yardly Gobion left the college and strolled down the Broad in the moonlight.

He had, as usual, made a sensation.

They had been discussing a social question, and though what knowledge of the matter he had came as much from intuition as experience, he spoke well and brilliantly, and now lit his cigarette with a pleasing sense of strength and nerve running through him. The sunshine of applause seemed to warm his impressionable brain, to make it expand with the power of receiving and mentally recording more vivid impressions. He had a pleasing consciousness of being very young and very interesting.

He was wonderfully quick and sympathetic in his perceptions, and he could see that every one of the good-natured men at the debate was thinking what a clever fellow he was.

He felt instinctively how all his carefully-studied tricks of manner and personal eccentricities told. The big football-playing, warm-hearted undergraduates admired him for his soft felt hat, his terra-cotta tie, his way of arranging his hands when he sat down, and his epigrams.

They imagined that all these things were the outcroppings of a distinctive personality, and indeed these little poses would have deceived, and very often did, far cleverer persons than they were.

To-night he had said in his speech of a certain genial and popular social reformer that he was a "doctrinaire with a touch of Corney Grain grafted on to a polemic attitude," and already in the Common Room they were chuckling over what they thought was a happy piece of impromptu caricature.

Gobion sauntered down the Broad and Turl to the college gates, and when he knocked in found several letters waiting for him in the lodge. He took them up to his rooms, turned on the light (they have electric light at Exeter), and arranged them in a row on the table. Then he turned and looked at himself in the glass. His hand shook till he had had some brandy, and he was several minutes moving restlessly about the room, putting on a blazer, and placing some stray books back on the shelves, before he sat down to read the first letter. He toyed about with it for some minutes, afraid to open it.

Outside in the quad a wine party were shouting and singing, their voices echoing strangely in the still winter night, their drunken shouts seeming to be mellowed and made musical by the ancient buildings. At last, with a quick nervous look round the room, he tore open the envelope and began to read. Without any heading the letter began:—

"Bassington Vicarage,

"*Sunday Night.*

"I have heard from Dr. Fletcher that you are suspected to be carrying on an intrigue with a low woman in Oxford; that you have not passed a single examination, and that you consistently fritter away your time in speaking at debating societies, and are in the habit of being frequently intoxicated.

"You have written me accounts of your progress and work at the University, which, on investigation, I find to be simply a tissue of lies.

"I have had bills for large amounts sent to me during the last few weeks from tradesmen, saying that they find it impossible to get any money from you, and that you ignore their communications. You have had splendid opportunities, a good name, with abilities above the average, and I believed that you would have done me credit. Your deceit and cruelty have broken my heart.

"I shall do nothing further for you, and you must make your own plans for the future.

"I shall not help you in any way.

"Your unhappy

"Father."

He got up and had some more brandy, walking about the room. "I knew the old fool would find out soon. My God, though, it's rather sudden. I haven't twopence in the world, and the High Church people are beginning to smell a rat. Damn this collar—it's tight...." He tore it off, smashing the head of the stud, which rolled under the fender with a sharp metallic click. After a time he sat down again. The feeling of ruin was already passing away, and his face lost its sweetness and youth, while a sharp keen look took its place—the look that he wore when at night he was alone and plotting, a haggard, old look which no one ever saw but Condamine or Sturtevant.

He took up the next letter, a small envelope addressed in a girl's hand:—

"Westcott,

"Wooton Woods."

"Dearest Caradoc,—You cannot think how delighted I was to get your letter on Saturday. I have been thinking of you a good deal the last two or three weeks, and wondering why you did not write.

"Had you forgotten all about me? I expect so, but there is some excuse for you, as you must meet heaps of *pretty* girls in Oxford. Do write me a nice long letter soon—a *nice* letter, you know.
"Good-bye, dearest—
"Your *very* loving

"Goodie.

"P.S.—Excuse scrawl."

The hard, keen expression faded away, his eyes filling with tears, while the light played caressingly on his face and tumbled hair.

It was his one pure affection, an attachment for a dear little girl of seventeen, a clergyman's daughter in the country. He thought of the evening walks in the sweet summer meadows, when the "mellow lin lan lone of evening bells" ringing for evensong floated over the corn. He remembered how her hair had touched his face, and how she had whispered "dearest."

And then the thoughts of all the other women in Oxford and London came crowding into his brain. The hot kisses, the suppers and patchouli-scented rooms, the slang and high tinkling laughter. His brow wrinkled up with pain as he walked up and down the room, filled with a supreme self-pity.

He remembered half unconsciously that Charles Ravenshoe had said, "Will the dawn never come? Will the dawn never come?" and he began to moan it aloud, with an æsthetic pleasure in the feeling of desolation and melancholy wasted hours—"will the dawn *never* come?" He came opposite the looking- glass, and was struck with the beauty of his own face, sad and pure. He gazed intently for a minute or two, then his features relaxed, and he breathed hard and smiled, murmuring, "Ah, well, a little purity and romance whip the jaded soul pleasantly. Goodie is a darling, and I love her, but still the others were amusing and piquant. They were the iota subscripts of love!"

There were still two more letters to be opened. One ran:—

"162a, Strand, W.C.

"Dear Mr. Yardly Gobion,—I shall be glad if you will do us a review of Canon Emeric's new book, *Art and Religion*. We can take half a column —leaded type; and shall be glad to have the copy by Friday at the latest. Are you going to be in town at all soon? If so I shall possibly be able to give you work on *The Pilgrim*, as we want an extra man, and I have been quite satisfied with what you have done for us so far.

"Please do not be later than Friday with the review.

"Believe me, yours very truly,

"James Heath."

"Just what I want! good—I like *The Pilgrim*, it's smart—this is luck. I suppose they like my 'occ' reviews. Heath always likes work that keeps cleverly on the border, and I imagine that I have shown him how to be realistic without being indelicate. Dear old Providence manages things very well after all. I really must do a short drink on the strength of this."

And he had some more brandy.

The last letter was simply a breakfast invitation.

He sat up for half an hour more making plans for the morrow, finally deciding to borrow all the money he could and go up to town in the afternoon.

It was now nearly half-past one, and the excitement of the debate and later of the letters had left him shaking and tired, so he turned out the light and went into his bedroom. Just as he was closing the door of communication, he noticed by the firelight that his father's letter had dropped on the hearthrug, and he went back, putting it in the fire with a grin.

Then the door shut, and the room was silent.

CHAPTER II.

SCOTT IS LONELY.

Bravery Reginald Scott, of Merton, was one of Gobion's chief admirers. He thought that no one was so clever or so good, and felt sure that his friend's traducers—and they were many—had never really got down below the crust of cynicism and surface immorality of mind as he had done. He certainly knew that Gobion occasionally drank more than was good for him, but he put it down to misadventure more than taste.

He was a good young man, rather commonplace in intellect, but of a blameless life and an unsuspicious, happy temperament.

A man who had always been on the best of terms with an adoring family and a wealthy father, he ambled easily through life, enjoying everything, and being especially happy when he was worked up into an emotion by a poem or sunset.

Generally tethered in the shallows of everyday circumstances, his mind experienced undimmed delight in acute sensation.

He had one great motif running like a silver thread through his consciousness —his love for Gobion; and every night he humbly and earnestly prayed for him, kneeling at a little *prie-Dieu* painted green.

To him there had been something very sacred in his relations with this man. One night Gobion had stayed behind after a wine party, and had sat late, staring into the fire and talking simply and hopefully about the trials and temptations of a young man's life. Very frankly he had talked with a nobleness of ideal and breadth of thought that fascinated Scott and made him feel drawn close to this strange handsome boy who was so assured and so hopeful.

After that first night there had been others when they sat alone, and Gobion talked airily with a fantastic wealth of fancy and sweetness of expression.

Scott thought he could see in all this man's conversation a high purpose and a stainless purity, made the more obvious by attempts at concealment.

Then again, Gobion gave him the impression of being delightfully unworldly, with no idea of the value of money, for he would come to him unconcernedly and borrow ten pounds to get out of some scrape, with a careless freedom that seemed to point to an absolute childishness in money matters.

Scott always lent it, and gloried in the feeling that he was helping the friend of his soul, albeit that Gobion had had most of his available cash, and he knew his affairs were getting something precarious.

On the morning of the Wadham debate he lay in bed half dozing, with a pleasing sense of anticipation.

Gobion was coming to a *tête-á-tête* breakfast, and he wondered what he would talk about, whether he would wear what he called his "explicit" tie or that green suit which became him so well.

Not far away in Exeter, the object of his thoughts was getting up and carefully dressing. He was thinking over the part he would have to play at breakfast, and devising some way of breaking the news of his approaching flight, and thinking out a plan for getting as much money as he could to take him up to town.

He had finished his toilette, and was passing out of his bedroom when he noticed that he looked in capital health, and not at all anxious or unhappy enough for a ruined man.

Scott would doubtless never have noticed, but Gobion was nothing if not an artist, and had a hatred of incompleteness.

Accordingly, he pulled a box of water-colour paints out of a drawer in his writing table, and carefully pencilled two dark sepia lines under his eyes, several times sponging them off till he had got what he considered a proper effect.

About a quarter after nine Scott's bedroom door opened unceremoniously, and Gobion came in.

Scott jumped up.

"I'm beastly sorry, old man, to be so slack. I'll be up in a minute. Is brekker in?"

"Never mind, old man; I'll go back into the next room and wait."

When breakfast was brought they sat for a time in silence. Then Gobion spoke.

"Old man, the game's up."

"What!"

"I'm done—utterly."

"What do you mean?"

"Well, you know how unlucky I have been in exams, and what a small allowance I have always had?"

"Yes."

"Well, the guvnor has written saying that I am idle and hopeless, and has taken my name off the books and refused to have anything more to do with me."

Scott gasped. "Oh, Lord, I *am* so sorry—dear old man—never mind, remember we promised to stick to each other. Now let's talk it over. What do you propose to do?"

"I shall go up to town this afternoon if I can get some money. I have had some work offered me on *The Pilgrim,* and I am sure to get along somehow."

"Of course you will, old man, you always succeed—look here, have you got any 'oof?"

"Not a penny."

"Well, I've got about twenty pounds I don't want. You had better take them."

"Thanks awfully, old chap, but I don't think I will, I owe you too much as it is. I don't know when I shall be able to repay you."

"Oh, but do, old man, you *must* have some cash."

"Well, if——"

"Ah, I knew you wouldn't mind; let me write you a cheque, you can cash it at the Old Bank this morning."

And he got out his cheque-book and wrote it. Gobion took it without saying anything, but he stretched out his hand and looked him in the face. With wonderful intuition he knew exactly what the other expected, and Scott felt repaid by his warm grasp and silence, which, as Gobion expected, he mistook for emotion.

After a melancholy cigarette Gobion got up and said, "You'll come and see me off, of course? I've got a lot to do, but I will have tea here at four and you can come to the station after. My train leaves at 5.30. Do you mind telling Robertson and Fleming, and anyone else you come across, and getting them to come too?"

The sun was shining when Gobion got out, and he thought that his first success was a good omen for the future. He strolled up to the bank feeling well fed and happy, and the strangeness of his position induced a pleasing sense of excitement and anticipation. He liked to think that he would be in the Strand that same evening.

When he had got his money he went to Condamine's rooms in Grove Street, where, as he expected, he found Sturtevant. He wore the yellow silk tie this morning.

They were having breakfast, and Condamine, unwashed and unshaven, dressed in pyjamas, with his feet thrust into a venerable pair of dancing pumps with the bows gone, was indignantly holding forth on the unapproachable manner of some barmaid or other whom he had discovered.

Gobion took the proffered drink. "First this mornin'," he said, and then, "I'm going down to-day."

"Game up?" said Sturtevant. These men were never excited.

"Exactly. When shall you be up?"

"I shall be in my chambers, 6, Middle Temple Lane, in three weeks' time, ready for a campaign in Fleet Street; we'll work together."

"Right you are; but aren't you afraid of my queering your pitch?"

"I'll take the risk of that. When do you go?"

"Five-thirty train."

"Shall we come to the station?" said Condamine.

"No, don't, the 'good' set will be there, and as I hope to carry off most of their spare cash, I think it would be wiser to depart in the odour of sanctity, and you'd rather spoil it."

"Right oh!" said the president, using one of his favourite phrases, and then raising his glass to his lips, "The old toast?"

"The old toast," said Condamine, "the three consonants"; and they drank it and said good-bye.

These three men were bound together by many an orgie, many a shady intrigue and modest swindle; they had no illusions about each other, but now they all felt a keen pang of regret that their little society was to be broken up.

Gobion went out feeling sorry, but he had too much to do to indulge in sentiment. He hoped to turn his twenty pounds into forty before lunch.

As he went into the High, bells were ringing, tutors hurrying along, and men going to lectures in cap and gown. A group of men in "Newmarkets" came round the corner of King Edward Street, going to hunt, and nearly knocked down Professor Max Müller, who was carrying a brown paper parcel and walking very fast. The Jap shop-girl in a new hat passed with a smile, and a Christchurch man and rowing blue came out of the "Mitre," where, no doubt, he had been looking over the morning paper, and gleaning information about his own state of health. The scene was bright and animated, and the winter's sun cast a glamour over everything.

Nearly every other man stopped and spoke to Gobion, and he felt strangely moved to think that he would soon be out of it all and forgotten.

He turned into the stable-yard of the "Bell," and stood there for a moment irresolutely, frowning, and then with a quick movement went into the private bar.

It was quite empty of customers, and a girl sat before the fire with her feet on the fender reading a novel.

She jumped up when Gobion came in, and he put his arm round her waist and kissed her. She was a pretty, fresh-looking girl, and would have been prettier still if she had not so obviously darkened her eyelashes with a burnt hairpin.

Gobion sat down on the chair, and pulled her on to his knee, smiling at her, and puffing rings of cigarette smoke at her.

She settled herself comfortably, leaning back in his arms, and began to rattle away in a rather high-pitched voice about a raid of the proctors the night before.

As is the habit of the more "swagger" sort of barmaid, she used the word "awfully" (with the accent on the *aw*) once or twice in nearly every sentence, and it was curious to hear how glibly the Varsity slang and contractions slipped from her.

He played with a loose curl of hair, thinking what a pretty little fool she was.

"Maudie dear, I'm going away."

"Do you mean for *good*?"

"I'm afraid so, darling."

She opened her eyes wide and puckered up her forehead. She looked very nice, and he kissed her again.

"I don't understand," she said.

"Well, the fact is the guvnor has stopped supplies, and I'm sent down."

"And you're going to leave *me*?… and we've had such an awfully jolly time … oh, you cruel boy!"

And she began to sob.

He grinned perplexedly over her head.

"… Never mind, dearest, I'll write to you and come down and see you soon."

"I don't know *what* I shall do…. I l-liked you s-so much better than the others…. *Don't* go."

"But, Maudie, I must. Look here, I will come in after lunch and arrange things properly. I'm in a fearful hurry now, and I shan't go till to-morrow."

"Really!"

"Oh, rather; now give me a B. and S. I really must depart."

She got up from his knee, and went behind the counter in the corner of the room.

"I'm going to have some first," she said.

"You're a naughty little girl!"

"Am I? you rather like it, don't you?"… She looked tempting when she smiled.

"May I?"

"You've had such a lot!"

"Just one to keep me going till after lunch."

"Stupid boy; well, there——"

"That was ve-ry nice. Good-bye for the present, dear."

She made a little mock curtsey. "I shall expect you at two … dear!"

He kissed his hand and shut the door, breathing a sigh of relief when he got outside.

"She won't see me again. I'm well out of that," he thought, his cheeks still burning with her hot kisses.

"Now for the worst ordeal."

Father Gray came out of the private chapel of the clergy-house in his cassock and biretta.

He had been hearing the somewhat long confession of an innocuous but unnecessary Keble man, and felt inclined to be irritable. He met Gobion going up to his room.

His pale lined face lighted up—most people's faces did when they saw Gobion.

"You here, dear boy? Come in—come into my room."

He opened the door, and went in with his hand on Gobion's shoulder. The room was panelled in dark green, and warmed by a gas stove. The shelves were filled with books, and books littered the floor and chairs, and even invaded two big writing-tables covered with papers. Over the mantelpiece was hung a print of Andrea Mantegna's Adoration of the Magi. On the wall opposite was a great crucifix, while underneath it was a little shelf covered with worn black velvet, with two silver candlesticks standing on it.

Behind a green curtain stood an iron frame, holding a basin and jug of water.

All the great Anglican priests had been in that room at one time or another.

From it retreats were organized, the innumerable squabbles of the various sisterhoods settled, and arrangements made for the private confession of High Church bishops who required a tonic.

In fact, this business-like little room was in itself the head-quarters of what that amusing print *The English Churchman* would call "the most Romanizing members of the Ritualistic party."

They sat down. Father Gray said, "You have something to tell me?"

"Yes," Gobion answered sadly, "I am ruined."

"Oh, come, come! What's all this? A boy like you can't be ruined."

"My father has put the last touch to his unkindness, and quite given me up. You know how I have tried to work and lead a decent life; but he won't listen, and I'm going to work at journalism in London and take my chance."

"My poor boy, my poor boy!" And the old priest was silent.

Then he said, "Do you think you can keep yourself?"

"I am sure I can, if only I can tide over the first three months. I expect it will be very hard at first though."

"Have you any money?"

"No; and I am heavily in debt into the bargain."

"Oh, well, well, we must manage all that somehow. I won't let you starve. You have always been so frank with me, and told me all your troubles. We understand one another; you must let me lend you some for a time."

"It's awfully good of you."

"Oh, nonsense, these things are nothing between you and me; here is a cheque for five-and-twenty pounds, that will keep you going for a month or two. You know I'm not exactly a poor man. Now you'll stay to lunch, the Bishop's coming."

"No, thanks, I won't stay, I'll say good-bye now; I want to be alone and think. Thank you so very much; I haven't led a very happy life at Oxford, but I *have* tried … and you've been so kind…. I am afraid I am utterly unworthy of it all"; and his voice trembled artistically.

"My boy," said the old man, and his face shone, "you have been foolish, and wasted your chances. You have not been very bad. Thank God that you are pure and don't drink. God bless you—go out and prosper, keep innocence; now good-bye, good-bye"; and he made the sign of the cross in the air.

Gobion got outside somehow, feeling rather unwell. He did not feel particularly pleased with his success at first, but the sun, and the crowd of people, and the wonderful irrepressible gaiety of the High just before lunch on a fine day cheered him up; and he cashed the second cheque, enjoying the look of surprise on the clerk's face, which was an unusual thing, because bank clerks, though always discourteous, are seldom surprised.

Then he went back to college and packed his portmanteau.

He left most of his books, and took only clothes and things that did not require much room. Scott would send up the heavy things after him. He told his scout he was going down for a few days, and that Mr. Scott of Merton would forward all letters. He knew that if his intended departure became known his creditors would rush to the Rector, and he would probably be detained.

He lingered over lunch, making an excellent meal, drinking a good deal of brandy, and thinking over the position. As far as he could see things were not so very bad; he could probably earn enough by journalism to keep him, and he had forty-five pounds in his pocket, while the pleasures of London awaited him.

He lay back in an armchair, taking deep draughts of hot cigarette smoke into his lungs, smiling at the idea of his morning's work, and wondering how he had done it—analyzing and dissecting his own fascination.

It is a curious thing that the more evil we are the more intensely we are absorbed in our own personality. The clever scoundrel is always an egotist; and Gobion liked nothing better than to admire himself quietly and dispassionately.

Leaning back half asleep, looking lazily at the purring, spitting fire, his thoughts turned swiftly into memories, and a vista of the last few years opened up before him.

He saw himself a boy of fifteen, keenly sensitive and inordinately vain. He remembered how his eager hunger for admiration had led him to pose even to his father and mother; how, when he found out he was clever, he used to lie carefully to conceal his misdoings from them. Gradually and slowly he had grown more evil and more bitter at the narrowness which misunderstood him.

When love had gone the deterioration was more marked, and he threw himself into grossness. His imagination was too quick and vivid to let him live in vice wholly without remorse, and every now and again he wildly and passionately confessed his sins and turned his back on them, as he thought, for ever. Then after a week or two the emotional fervour of repentance would wear off, and he would plunge more deeply into vice, and lead a jolly, wicked life.

But keenest and most poignant of all his memories were the quiet summer evenings with Scott or Taylor, when the windows were open, and the long days sank gently into painted evenings. It was at times like these, when all the charm and mellow beauty of evening floating down on the ancient town of spires sensuously bade him forget the life he was leading, and thrilled all the poetry and fervour in him, that he would talk simply and beautifully, and stir his friends into a passion of enthusiasm by his ideals. The gloriousness of youth bound them all together, and in the summer quiet of some old-world college garden the wolf and the lambs held sweet converse, generally in the chosen language of that university exclusiveness which is at once so pretty and so delightful, so impotent, and yet full of possibilities. Detached scenes rose up … the almost painful æsthetic pleasure he had felt when he had gone to evensong at Magdalen with Scott, and the scent of the summer seemed to penetrate and be felt through the solemn singing and sonorous booming of the lessons.

… The High by moonlight—the most fairy-like scene in Europe. Scott's arm in his, and the grey towers shimmering in the quivering moonspun air.

A black cloud of horror and despair came down on him. He saw himself as he was. For once he dared to look at his own evil heart, and no light came to him in that dark hour.

A little before half-past five, nine or ten men stood on the platform of the Great Western station talking together.

A group of what Gobion called the "good" set had come to see him go.

They stood round, sorrowfully pressing him to write and let them know how he got on.

Fleming went to the bookstall and bought a great bundle of papers and magazines, and Scott appeared at the door of the refreshment-room laden with sandwiches and a flask of sherry.

They shook hands all round; it was the last time most of them saw him. Sadly they said good-bye, and took a last look at his clear-cut face.

Scott claimed the last adieu, and leant into the carriage, pressing Gobion's hand, afraid to speak. Gobion felt a horrible remorse, but he choked down his emotion by an enormous effort of will.

The train began to move.

"God bless you, God bless you, old un," said Scott hoarsely.

"An epithet is the conclusion of a syllogism," said Gobion to himself, lighting a cigarette as the train glided out of the station.

So he went his way, and they saw him no more.

CHAPTER III.

INITIATION.

Gobion went to the Grosvenor Hotel and dressed for dinner. Never before had he been so free, so unrestrained. A most pleasurable feeling of excitement possessed him.

He knew he could venture where another man would fail; he had fascination, resource—he was utterly unscrupulous; it was almost pleasingly dramatic.

He stood in the hall after dinner and lit a cigarette, watching the crowd of well-dressed people on the lounges round the wall, enjoying their after-dinner coffee.

The excellent dinner he had eaten still wanted the final climax of coffee, and sitting down in an armchair he ordered some.

The dreamy content of a well-fed, but not over-fed, man beamed from him. What should he do?—a music-hall perhaps—he could almost have laughed aloud in pure amusement and delight at his freedom.

A man sitting near asked him for a match, and they began to talk in the idle desultory way of two chance acquaintances, making remarks about the people sitting round.

A big, yellow-haired girl was talking and laughing in loud tones on the other side of the room, clattering her fan with, it seemed to Gobion, quite unnecessary noise.

"Who is that person?" he said.

"Which?"

"The girl with the bun, by the potted palm."

"Oh," said the stranger, "that is Lady Mary Aiden Hibbert; she is of a rather buoyant disposition."

"Not to say *Tom* buoyant," said Gobion, punning lazily; "she seems of an amiable complexion."

"My dear sir, complexion of both kinds is influenced by cosmetics, not by character."

"I perceive you are a cynic."

"Possibly," said the other in a meditative tone; "yet not so much of a cynic as a man in quest of sensations.”

“A society journalist?”

“No, merely a man who has become tired of the higher immorality, and wants something else to do.”

Gobion laughed and got up. “I’m going to the Palace for an hour or two.”

“May I come?” said the stranger; “my name is Jones.”

“Please do. I am called Yardly Gobion. I shouldn’t like to be called Jones, it’s not a pretty name.”

The other smiled, he was not vexed; Gobion knew his man. They drove swiftly to the Palace through the lighted streets, talking a little on the way. When they went into the stalls the hysterio-comic of the hour was leaping round the stage in frenzied pirouettes between the verses of her song.

The suggestive music of the dance pulsed through the audience, and when the time sank into the rhythm of the verse, they sat back in their seats with expectant eyes, and a little sigh of delight and anticipation.

Miss Mace, in her song “It’s a Family Characteristic,” was the talk of London. The *risquè* nature of the words, her wonderful art in singing them, her naughty eyes, the twitching of her somewhat large mouth—all the lewd papers of the baser sort yelled over her in ecstasy every Wednesday morning.

“I wonder what they pay her a week,” said Mr. Jones.

Gobion hadn’t an idea, but he said “sixty pounds” confidently.

“Really! She certainly is very clever.”

“The best thing I find about her is that she is in wonderful sympathy with her audience, especially too when she is drunk—much funnier then.”

“Imagine how often the average faddist would invoke the Deity during her turn,” said the stranger something sententiously.

“His deity, you mean,” answered Gobion. “The average man of the *Echo*-reading type thinks God is a policeman in the service of the Purity party.”

“You coruscate; let us go to the American bar.”

“That’s a good idea; the presiding gentleman who makes the drinks is an artist. The mingled science and art with which he compounds whimsical beverages is wonderful. Half of him seems impulse and nervous force as he rattles the pounded ice and flourishes the glasses, while the other half looks in and puts the finishing touches.”

"You talk nonsense very pleasantly," said Mr. Jones. "What will you have?"

"Oh! a sherry cobbler, please, *with* straws."

"Are you a connoisseur in drinks?"

"Not yet; I hope to be."

"I will take you to a place where you may learn."

"Please do; drinks are more than a cult, they are a science. To a man I knew at Oxford they were a religion." He was thinking of Condamine.

"There are so many religions nowadays."

"Yes; the sham of yesterday takes an alias and calls itself the religion of the future."

"I hate the faddist."

"What *do* you like?"

"I haven't many likes left now. I like to be amused as much as possible."

After a time they left the music-hall, and while they were walking through clubland the stranger permitted himself more freedom of expression, talking cynically. He was a middle-aged man, and Gobion amused him immensely.

"How badly brought up you must have been," he said to him.

"Why, what makes you think so?"

"You vibrate so quickly to my views, and I am not considered orthodox."

"Well, I was not so much badly brought up, as left to myself. My father's pedigree claimed a larger share of his attention than his progeny. I was an accident in the domestic arrangements."

"He must be a strange person."

"He is. I always suspect my predisposition to shady pleasures is hereditary, although he is a parson."

"It's quite often the case that a repentant rake takes Orders from a mere revulsion to asceticism. And your mother?"

"A nonentity with most seductive hair."

While talking, they had arrived at the Park, and were turning home to the hotel in the fresh night air. Gobion knew that he had been smart, perhaps smarter than usual, but he did not know what impression he had made. The stranger was a man outside his experience. Accustomed as Gobion was, in the light of Oxford experience, to feel that *he* was the cynic and man of the world, he was somewhat doubtful of a man who appeared to him to be a realization of what he might himself become. Cynicism, he thought, is now my plaything; it is this man's master, and he has lost the savours of life. I wonder if Father Gray was right. He often said that up to thirty a man might be happy with no moral sense; but after——

He saw dimly a foreshortened view of the future. It was on this night that the confidence in his own ability to be happy in evil began to be a little undermined. This chance meeting with a man weary of life, and not interested in death, a man with an aching, futile soul, whom he never saw again, was fraught with tremendous importance to his future career. On this his first night in London the seeds were sown which led to the final pose in Houndsditch.

A celebrated lady novelist (she is now in Colney Hatch, but very clever) once said to the writer of these memoirs that literature, or rather journalism, is little more than a big game of bluff. Her remark was quite true. The art of the thing consists in getting the keynote of twenty different publics, and writing on those lines for the twenty different papers that represent their views.

This is not the way to make a reputation, but it is certainly one of the ways in which the literary adventurer may make a certain amount of money. Gobion knew this well. The conquest was mean and the reward not far from meagre; but at his age and with his past he could not hope for much more, and there was a bustling excitement in it which seemed to him most desirable.

He could not specialize; he had no fixed opinions. It was impossible for him to take up a decided line in his work.

At Oxford the exigencies of his career had forced him to have no opinions, but simply to adopt the policy of the set he happened to be with. He belonged to no party, and in moral views, though he was apparently in agreement with both, he titillated the men of a clean and decent life, and amused their opposites, while he borrowed money from both with a cheerful impartiality. As far as he could dispassionately reckon them up, his mental assets were a felicity and facility of expression, more or less wide reading, and a power of intuition and knowledge of the public mind that was almost devilish in its infallibility.

After breakfast next morning, that meal so dear (in more senses than one) to the undergraduate, obviously the first thing to be done was to secure a place to dwell in. It was not wise to stay on at the hotel a moment longer than was necessary; the expense was too great. He thought at once of the Temple. It was a good address, and near most things. He knew enough of London to understand that Bloomsbury was clerk-land, and though cheap, quite impossible. Westminster was better, but not quite central enough. Finally, after some trouble, he took two first-floor rooms in one of the quiet streets running from the Fleet Street end of the Strand to the Embankment. They were well-furnished bachelor rooms, with a low window-seat from which a glimpse could be caught of red-sailed barges with yellow masts of pitch-pine floating slowly down the tide, while on late wintry afternoons the sunsets stained the brown water with a grim and sullen glory.

Gobion had a lurking hope that he might meet the comic landlady that Mr. Farjeon writes about so nicely in the flesh. He was doomed to disappointment. The person, called Mrs. Daily, who owned the house had no peculiarities, and nothing to suggest the type he was in search of save rotundity of form. He was loth to think the comic landlady was a fabulous monster, or an extinct one— the lady who says, "Which Mister Jones come tight last blessed hevening has hever was, and which I 'ad to bump 'is 'edd on the stairs to keep 'im quiet while the girl and I 'elped 'im up to the third floor back." Was she really fabulous? It was a sorrowful reflection.

The same day that he took the rooms he moved from the West and took possession. He had dined at the hotel before he left, and when he had unpacked his portmanteaux he sat before the fire feeling horribly dull and uneasy.

He was not inclined to go out to a theatre or bar, and the men he knew in town, mostly journalists, were all hard at work now in Fleet Street.

The sensation of *ennui* was new to him, and at first quite overbearing. Gobion was in personal matters strong-willed, and after a time this trained faculty of will helped him, and, with an effort almost heroic in its strength, he sat down at the table and began to review a book for *The Pilgrim*. It was a collection of essays by a well-known priest on some doctrinal aspects of church teaching that he had before him, and it was sent to him partly because he was known to have had some connection with the High Church party, and the editor assumed that he would have enough superficial knowledge of the subject to write a clever and flippant review.

The Pilgrim had been bought at a low ebb in its fortunes by its present editor, James Heath, for a thousand pounds, lock, stock, and barrel. Before it came into his hands it was an unsavoury little print, which published little else but impressionist criticisms of the music-halls and fulsome reviews of evil books, under the direction of a man who was a personified animal passion roughly clothed in flesh.

Now it was all changed. The tone of *The Pilgrim* was immoral as before, and the column headed "The Pilgrim's Scrip" as grossly personal as ever, but the personalities were more artistic, the immorality the immorality of culture.

The paper was never low. The sale was good, for all the young men and women who considered themselves clever, and who, under the comprehensive shield of "soul," sucked poison from strange flowers, bought it and quoted it.

Heath was smart and cynical in his conduct of the paper, though in private life he lived at Putney, collected stamps, and read Miss Braddon's novels to his wife after dinner. He knew quite well that realism was mechanism, and he never welcomed photography as art, but as the people who bought his literary wares did not understand these things he never enlightened them, which was natural.

The book that Gobion was reviewing he had entrusted to him willingly. He was an Oxford man himself, and still kept up some communication with his friends there, and he had heard indirectly that Gobion had received various benefits from the High Church party. His knowledge of Gobion taught him that he would do a delightfully clever and malicious review.

The clergyman who had written the book was a rather noisy Anglican divine, who preached the gospel of unity in art and religion at the top of his voice. He deprecated and eloquently denounced the new literature of the day. As *The Pilgrim* was the outward and visible head of what Canon Emeric denounced as very little short of devilish, Heath was naturally anxious that the review should, in journalistic phrase, "crab" the sale of the book among his readers.

Now this Canon Emeric had met Gobion at a garden party, and found him well informed in the history of his campaign against art for art's sake. Finding that Gobion agreed with his views, he had asked him as a special favour to call on his son, who had just come up to Christchurch from Marlborough. Gobion did call, and asked the youth to meet Sturtevant, and the poor boy, dazzled by being in the society of men of whom he heard everyone talking, made a fool of himself and came to utter grief, much to the pecuniary benefit of Condamine, Sturtevant, and Gobion. It was a disgraceful affair, and though some rather acrimonious correspondence had passed between the Canon and Gobion, the matter had been hushed up.

When Gobion got well into his work the ennui passed away and he worked hard, turning out a very clever and caustic review. To the pleasure of creation, always a keen one with him, was added the delight of writing something which, if he saw it, would pain his adversary grievously. And Gobion meant to take very good care that he *did* see it.

He ended the column by saying:—

"Whether these essays were worth writing is of course a question which lies between Canon Emeric and his publisher. That they are not worth reading we have no hesitation in saying.

"If anyone were so childish as to take the advice given in this book seriously, he would find that

It took him about two hours to produce the criticism in its finished state, and then he began to have a last smoke before going to bed. As with so many men, he found that at no time did his ideas come so rapidly, or shape themselves so well, as during the smoking of that last cigarette.

The fire was blazing, and he drew his chair up closer, leaning back and enjoying in every nerve a moment of intense physical ease.

There was no more innocent picture to be found in London than the well-furnished room lit by the dancing firelight, with the handsome young man in the chair lazily watching the blue cigarette smoke slowly twisting itself into strange fantastic shapes. The powers of Asmodeus were here a failure.

Next day, when he had written to his Oxford friends and to Marjorie Lovering, his sweetheart in the country, he went to *The Pilgrim* office with his review and saw Heath. The two editorial rooms were on the second floor looking out into the Strand. Big bare places littered with paper, cigarette ends, and type-written copy, with none of the tape machines, telephones, and fire- calls that are found in the offices of a daily. Heath was seated at a writing- table "making up" the issue for the week, while his assistant, a man named Wild, was looking through a batch of cuttings from Romeike's in the hope of finding what he called "spicy pars" for the front page. Gobion was well received, and after he had explained that he was going to stay in town, and was open for any amount of work, he was offered a permanent salary of two pounds ten shillings a week, to do half the reviewing for the paper. Naturally he accepted at once, and was pleased at his good luck, for though the pay was small it was regular.

Heath was a very large, fat man, with no hair on his face, and a quick, nervous smile which ended high in the pendant flabbiness of his cheeks. He was well and fashionably dressed in dark grey, the frock coat, tight-fitting as it was, making his vast size and huge hips seem the more noticeable. He was smoking a cigar, and gave Gobion one.

It was lunch time when the bargain was concluded, and Gobion, Wild, and Heath went out together. Gobion, who, obeying the precept of Iago, had put money in his purse, asked them to lunch with him at Romano's. Heath laughed.

"My *dear* Yardly Gobion, lunch at Romano's! No thanks; it would cost you five pounds and be far too respectable. No, you shall certainly pay for the lunch—eh Wild?—but I will show you where to get it."

He turned up a side street and entered a small court, not far from the stage door of the Lyceum, at the end of which was a door. They went in and found a suite of three largish rooms opening one out of the other. The first was fitted up as a restaurant, while the other two were smoking-lounges with a bar in each. Comfort, brutal unæsthetic comfort, was the most obvious thing in all three rooms. The chairs were comfortable, the carpets soft, while big cheery fires burnt in the open grates. No one was in the dining-room, but through the half-open curtains, which separated the lounge from the dining-room, came snatches of conversation, the sound of soda-water corks, and the shrill laughter of a London barmaid, than which few things are more unpleasant.

The three journalists sat down at a table by the fire, and a waiter brought the menu.

Mr. Heath's rather impassive face lighted up, and he read the list eagerly. Eating and drinking were of tremendous importance to him.

The food was ordered, and Gobion asked them what they would drink. Heath, with a sublime disregard for bulk, ordered lager; the other two, simple "halves" of bitter. While the meal was in progress a man came in from a side door. Heath called him, introducing him to Gobion as Mr. Hamilton, the owner of the place.

Wild explained to Gobion that he was now free of the "copy shop." "You see," said he, "this is a place almost entirely used by journalists of a non- political kind. Everyone knows everyone else, and Hamilton knows us all by name. An outsider who wanders in here is not encouraged to repeat his visit, unless he is vouched for by someone, for the place is really more like a club than a public bar."

After lunch they went into the lounge, which was filled with men, mostly young, who all seemed to know one another by their Christian names. Heath was hailed cordially.

A man sitting on the table stood up, and said theatrically, "Enter the Pilgrim, arch-druid of the loving Mountain—slow music. Well, my fat friend, what wicked scandal do you come fresh from concocting? What lewd pars are even now in the copy box at 162, Strand?"

The Pilgrim grinned. "Gentlemen, let me introduce my latest permanent recruit, Mr. Yardly Gobion. He has just been sent down from Exeter." Gobion was welcomed as a brother, and in half an hour had taken up his favourite position on the hearthrug.

Exerting himself to the utmost, he found he could produce much the same impression as he did in Oxford, and he was a pronounced success in perhaps one of the most critical coteries in London.

They were critics of everything, criticism was in their veins, they lived on it; they were "the men who had failed in literature and art."

Every now and then a man or two on an evening paper would come in hastily for a drink, and there was a quick interchange of technicalities, a chorus of experts, sharp, clipped, allusive; the latest wire from the Central News, the newest story from the clubs, the smartest headline of the afternoon.

Gobion soon caught the note and was voted an acquisition. Although he was of a somewhat finer grain than most of these men, he recognized the type instantly. Cheap cynicism was the keynote of most of the conversation, and his lighter side revelled in it. Most complex of all men, he could suck pleasure from every shade of feeling. Lord Tennyson's beautiful line: "A glorious devil large in heart and brain," fitted him exactly. With his intellect he might have been a saint, instead of which he was sublime in nothing whatever. With the face of an angel, he loved goodness for its beauty, and sin for its excitement.

Before he left the "copy shop" he had picked up several good stories, and saw his way to at least half a dozen scandalous paragraphs, which he would send to a provincial paper with which he had some connection.

He went away, being pressed to come regularly, and Mr. Hamilton met him going out, expressing his pleasure at seeing any "friend of Mister Heath's and member of the fourth hestate, 'oping as the pleasure will be repeated." Not being a journalist, the worthy landlord had a high opinion of the press.

Gobion left with Wild, and they strolled down towards Fleet Street.

"Drop in at my place some evening, will you?" he said to his companion.

"Thanks very much. I will, certainly. You must come and look me up when you've time. I am at present sharing a flat with Blanche Huntley, whom you may have heard of. I suppose you don't mind?"

"I, my dear fellow? Rather not; delighted to come. Do you turn off here?"

"Yes, I'm going to the Temple station; good-bye."

Gobion had heard of Miss Huntley. "How very nasty some men are in their tastes," he thought; "it's all rather horrid. I'll go to evensong somewhere." Not the better, but the finer side of him woke up, and he felt the necessity of a quieting and poetic influence to counteract the clever sordidness of the afternoon. He took a cab to Pimlico, where he knew churches were plentiful, and after a little search found what he wanted not far from Victoria Station.

The church was only lit by the candles on the high altar and a solitary corona over the stall of the clergyman. Gobion was quite alone. The shadows and gloom of the building were thrown into a deeper gloom, an added mystery, by the radiance above. A young priest, of the earnest Cuddesdon type, walked in all alone, his steps echoing mournfully on the flagged chancel floor. He gave a slight start of pleasure when he saw that there was a congregation, a young man, too!—the poor curate had never before seen such a phenomenon at a weekday evensong.

They said the psalms together, Gobion's sweet voice echoing down the long, dark aisles.

The clergyman felt an instinctive sympathy. He saw that Gobion was feeling to the full the influence of the hour and place, the musical cadence of the verse, and he responded in his turn with a newer sense of the poetry of worship, throwing deep feeling into his voice. It was a keen, æsthetic pleasure to both of them, though the priest felt something more, but it put Gobion on good terms with himself at once. He had roused emotion of a sort, and the rousing seemed to sweep away the contamination of the day.

He bowed low to the distant crucifix on the altar on leaving the building, as a man who had tasted a sweet morsel, with shadowy and pleasant thoughts— the sense of a finer glory.

<hr>

CHAPTER IV.

THE CAMPAIGN.

When a few unconsidered trifles have been thrown out at score, to a middle-aged business man the world is a bundle of shares and bills receivable. To most young men it is a girl or several girls. For some girls it is a young man. For some other people it is a church, a bar, a coterie—for Yardly Gobion it was himself. Realizing this in every nerve, for the next few weeks he devoted himself to making acquaintances and impressions.

He did no writing beyond his weekly contribution to *The Pilgrim*, but went abroad and looked around, making himself a niche before he essayed anything further. He managed to get about to one or two rather decent houses, and greatly consolidated his position at the "copy shop." His idea was to keep quiet till Sturtevant came up to town, for he thought that very little could stand against such a combination. Accordingly he had a pleasant time for the next few weeks. His work did not take him more than four hours a day, and now that his circle of acquaintance was so much enlarged there was always plenty of amusement. He could always enjoy the small change of transient emotion by a visit to the church at Pimlico, where in the lonely services he felt (sometimes for nearly an hour) a sorrow at his life and a yearning for goodness.

His mental attitude on these occasions was a strange one, and one only found in people possessing the artistic temperament; for he seemed to stand aloof, and mourn over the grossness of some dear friend; he could detach his mind from his own personality, and feel an awful pity for his own dying soul. Then after these luxurious abandonments, these delightful lapses into religious sentimentality, he would seize on pleasure as a monkey seizes on a nut, finding an added zest in the pursuit of dissipation. One thing in some small degree he noticed, and that was that this alternation of attitude was slightly weakening his powers of taste. The sharpest edge of enjoyment seemed blunted.

One night, about a month after his arrival in town, he dined out in Chelsea with some friends, driving back to his rooms about eleven o'clock, very much in love with himself. On this particular evening he had not tried to be smart or clever. There had been several other ultra-modern young men there; and seeing that the hostess—a charming person—was wearied of their modernity and smart sayings, he affected quite another style, pleasing her by his deferential and chivalrous manner, the simplicity of his conversation. A fresh instance of his power always tickled his vanity, and he drove home down the Strand, his soul big with a hideous egoism.

He paid the driver liberally, for he was generous in all small matters, and opening the door with his latch-key went upstairs. He entered the room, and to his immeasurable surprise found it brilliantly lit with gas and candles. On the table was a half-empty bottle of champagne and a bedroom tumbler.

In a chair on the right side of the fireplace sat Sturtevant in his shirtsleeves, smoking a cigarette, while on the other side of the fire was a young lady dressed in the van of the fashion, also smoking. Her hat was off, and her hair was metallically golden.

"Where—the—devil—did you spring from?" said Gobion.

"My good friend—not before a lady, please," said Sturtevant with a grin.

The lady waved her cigarette in the air. "Spit it out, old man; don't mind me!" she said.

Gobion looked helplessly from the lady to Sturtevant and back again. These things were beyond him.

"Allow me," said Sturtevant. "Mr. Yardly Gobion, Miss—er—I don't know your name, my dear."

"Me?" said the young lady. "My name don't matter. I'm off; so long, boys."

"Will you explain?" said Gobion. "I am rather bewildered."

"Well, it's in this way. I got up to town about six this evening, and went to the Temple. I found my chambers in an excessively filthy state, with no fire, my laundress not expecting me till to-morrow. I dined at the 'Monico,' and met that damsel in Piccadilly; and, in short, we have been spending the evening under your hospitable roof, aided by a bottle of fizz from the 'Grecian.'"

"I see. Well, if you don't mind, old man, don't bring that sort in. I like them anywhere but in my rooms. A *demoiselle de trottoir* should stay——"

"On the *trottoir*—quite so. I won't offend again; only I wanted someone to amuse me, and I expected you'd be late. Now look here; can you put me up for the night? my chambers are in a horrible mess."

"Oh, I should think so; I'll ask the landlady."

At half-past eleven the next morning Gobion got up, after some trouble getting Sturtevant out of bed; and they began a composite meal which the president called "brunch" soon after twelve.

Some letters were waiting. One was a pathetic appeal from an Oxford tailor for "something on account." Gobion said "damn" (the Englishman's shortest prayer), and threw it into the fire. Another was a letter from Scott, strong, earnest, and loving. He passed it to Sturtevant, who read it and said, "Man seems to have kept it a little too long in a hot place. Trifle high, don't you think?"

The third ran:—

"My Dear Caradoc,

"Marjorie and I are coming up for a fortnight to stay with my mother in Kensington. We hope to see a good deal of you, as you say you have deserted Oxford for a time to take up some literary work in London.

"Marjorie tells me to say that you must meet our train—the 4.30 at Victoria, but don't put yourself out.

"Yours affectionately,

"Gerald Lovering."

"Hallo," said Gobion, "my girl's coming up!"

"Didn't know you had one; has she any money?"

"A little, I think, and her father looks on me as an eligible; he doesn't know I've been sent down, and I don't intend he shall. I have to meet the 4.30 this afternoon."

"Well, I wanted to talk over our plans some time to-day. When will you come to my chambers?"

"This evening, I should think. I must work till four; I've a novel to do for *The Pilgrim*, and I've not read a line yet."

"Oh, don't bother about that. 'Smell the paper-knife' instead; let's go to the 'copy shop.'"

"Afraid I can't; I must do it. Look here, I will come round about ten this evening. Don't be drunk."

"Right oh! I'll go back now and get my rooms into some sort of order."

He rolled a cigarette and roamed about the room, looking for his hat. "It's gone to the devil, I think," he said.

"In that case you'll find it again some day. There it is, though—under the sofa. I thought you didn't believe in the devil."

"Satan may be dead, as the hedonists think; but I expect someone still carries on the business."

When he had gone Gobion got to work, and wrote steadily till three, when he went to the "copy shop" to get something to eat. They kept him waiting some little time. Albert, the waiter, who was supposed to be smart in his profession, on this occasion hid his talent (no doubt in a napkin), and Gobion had only a minute to spare when he got to Victoria.

The train curved into the station and pulled up slowly. He made for the door of a first-class carriage where he saw Mr. Lovering getting out. The parson was a little man, all forehead and nose. When Gobion came up he was struggling with a bundle of rugs and umbrellas.

"Ah, dear boy, you have come then. So good of you. Get Marjorie out while I find our luggage."

Then Marjorie came down from the carriage, glowing with health and spirits, her dark eyes flashing when they saw Gobion.

"Dearest," he said. She put her little gloved hand into his, looking up in his face, while his blood ran faster through his veins.

"Caradoc, dear, it *is* so jolly to see you again; we are going to stay in London for over a fortnight, and you shall take me about everywhere. Oh, here's father."

The little man bustled up. He was one of those dreadful people whom a railway journey excites to a species of frenzy. He ran up and down the platform, dancing round the truck which held his baggage, holding a piece of paper in his hand, muttering, "One black bag—yes; two corded trunks—yes; one hat-box—yes; two boxes of ferns—yes; one bundle of rugs—y—NO! Marjorie! *where* are the rugs? Gobion, I *know* I had the rugs *after* we got out
—a big bundle with a striped red and green one on the outside."

"You're carrying it, aren't you, Mr. Lovering?"

"Dear me! so I am. How very stupid of me! Now if you will get a cab I should be so obliged—a four-wheeler, mind!"

Gobion secured one and came back, standing by Marjorie while the luggage was hoisted on the roof.

"I do hate a silly old four-wheeler!" she said.

"Never mind, dearest, soon we'll go about in a hansom together to your heart's content—jump in! May I call to-morrow, Mr. Lovering?"

"Yes, yes, dear boy—you know the address. Good-bye for the present."

Gobion left the station with a sense of *bien-être*. He remembered that he was not due at the Temple till ten, wondering what he should do with himself. Just as he was going out of the gates that rail off the station-yard from the street, a cab dashed up, the occupant evidently in haste to catch a train. Unfortunately, just as it was coming into the yard, the horse swerved and fell, and the man inside was shot out past Gobion, his head striking the curbstone with fearful force. Death was almost instantaneous. Gobion rushed up and lifted him in his arms, but it was of no use. In a short time two policemen came up, and after taking Gobion's name as a witness of the occurrence, placed the body on a stretcher, moving off with it followed by the crowd. The whole affair did not last ten minutes.

Gobion stood by himself staring at the blood on his clothes. He was moving away, when he saw the card-case of the dead man was lying in the gutter, where it had been jerked when he fell. He picked it up, giving a start of surprise when he saw the name Sir William Railton, a prominent member of the government in power.

All the horror of the scene passed away in a flash. He was a journalist pure and simple now, with an hour's start of any man in London. Hurriedly wiping his clothes, he ran over the road to Tinelli's, an Italian restaurant, and, ordering pens, paper, and a flask of Chianti, wrote furiously a brief account, about a quarter of a column long. He made five copies, and then got into a cab and drove hard to Fleet Street, leaving his card and an account at the news- office of each of the big dailies.

Then came the reaction, and he staggered home, faint with hard work and the horror of what he had seen. He put on another suit, not feeling himself till he had roused his spirits with a copious brandy and soda.

This instinct of the journalist is a curious thing; while it lasts it is a hot fever, brutal almost in its vehemence. A man possessed by it forgets everything but the fierce joy of his work, and a deep exaltation in the possession of exclusive news; but the reaction is bad for the nerves.

Sturtevant's chambers in the Temple were distinctly comfortable. A large room panelled in white, with doors opening round it into bedrooms. A gay Japanese screen protected a cosy corner by the fire, fitted up with a lounge, an armchair, two little tables, and a standard lamp. It was all more elaborate than his Oxford rooms, because at Oxford he was too well known for his position to depend on externals—while in London they were part of his stock-in-trade. It was a room in which laziness seemed a virtue, with numberless contrivances for comfort. Corners for elbows, shaded reading lamps, the best of tobacco, and a speaking-tube from the fireside to the outer passage of the chambers, so that on hearing a knock, Sturtevant could tell an unwelcome visitor that he was not at home, but was expected back about five, without opening the door.

"Now," he said, when they had settled down comfortably, "we shall be quite undisturbed all night. We have a good fire, tobacco, and drink of the best; let us seriously map out our little campaign."

"Take the evening papers first then," said Gobion. "Now there is the *Moon*, an organ devoted to playfully redressing wrongs. We will do an article for it on 'How Barmaids Live.' We can describe the horrors of their lot: a sleeping-room, 12 feet by 12, with six girls in it, and a window that won't open; the insults they are exposed to, *et cetera*."

"Do you think that will take?"

"Yes, and I'll tell you why. The ordinary beast who reads the *Moon* loves anything about a barmaid; they are his society."

"Where shall we get our facts?"

"Invent them, of course; there is no need for investigation. We can make it much more interesting without. Put it down: 'Barmaid—*Moon*.' Now we come to the *Resounder*. We must try quite a different line. It's a newspaper in a strait waistcoat, so to speak, and it's just been subsidized by the anti- gambling people. How would 'The Gambling Evil at the Universities' do? We could easily make some astounding revelations, and your name as president of the Union would have weight with the editor. What else is there?"

"Well, there's the *Evening Times* and the *Wire*," said Sturtevant.

"Yes; I think with them we must do short stories. I have three or four MSS. not yet printed which I will revise. All these things shall go in under your name, and I will invent two-stick pars about celebrities, and send three or four to each paper. For instance—

'It is not generally known that the Queen has a great liking for that very plebeian dish, tripe and onions. Indeed, so fond is Her Majesty of this succulent preparation, that a few sheep are always kept in the home paddocks of each of the royal residences to be in readiness if Her Majesty should suddenly express her desire. They are mountain bred, and are brought from the Highlands of Scotland as soon as they can travel without their dams.'

The British public love this kind of thing."

As Gobion suggested an article, one of them put it down on a piece of paper with the name of the journal to which they proposed to send it.

"I have a beautiful idea," said Sturtevant, after a pause.

"Yes?"

"Look here, you know all the High Church goings-on at Oxford, don't you?"

"Yes, but why?"

"There's a paper run in London called *The Protesting Protestant*, which discovers a new popish plot every week. Well, you supply me with enough facts and names to prove that there is widespread conspiracy going on to Romanize the undergraduates. See?"

"Ripping!"

"Yes, but wait a minute, the best part is to come. *Then* you go to the opposition High Church paper with a letter of introduction from Father Gray, and answer my attack and so on for the next few weeks, and divide the swag"; and he leaned back in his chair with a cigarette, with an air of conscious merit.

"This is more than smartness, Sturtevant," said Gobion, wagging his head at the tobacco-jar, "this is genius."

"We must be careful in what we say. It would be unpleasant to be imprisoned for a portion of our unnatural lives."

"Yes, we will hint more than we state. Style is the art of leaving out."

They went on like this for a good part of the night, arranging their plans, inventing new scandal, and making notes of useful lies.

Towards morning they had settled enough for a week's continuous work; only proposing, however, to deal with the less reputable papers, for they both knew well that there was no chance with any respectable sheet.

Just as Gobion was going, Sturtevant said, "What about typing? we can't send them in MSS."

"I think I can manage that," said Gobion; "a man called Wild, the sub-editor of *The Pilgrim*, is living with that girl Blanche Huntley, who was mixed up in the Wrampling case. She used to be a typewriter, and she has a machine still. Moreover she'd be glad to earn a pound or two for pocket money; Wild isn't generous. I wonder, by the way, if any of the things we propose to write are true?"

"Possibly; nature is always committing a breach of promise against the journalist."

They arranged not to begin the work till the Friday morning, as Gobion wished to have a day to spend with Marjorie.

In the morning he called in Kensington, and Mr. Lovering, with a chilly Christian smile, in which perchance lingered some reminiscence of his youth, left the two young people together.

Soon after, Gobion was sitting at Marjorie's side, with his arm round her waist and her head delightfully near his. Melodiously he whispered his joy at seeing her again, holding her little, tender, perfumed hand. He called forth all his powers of pleasing, and paid her delicate compliments, like kisses through a veil, compliments such as girls love, the refinements of adoration arranged neatly in a *bouquet*.

Marjorie was a damsel of many flirtatious loves, though perhaps Gobion was her especial favourite, he was so extremely good-looking; but she was the sort of girl that took nothing but chocolates seriously. As her mother had died when she was quite young, she had been sent to a boarding school, and had caught the note. She had no mind—girls of this sort never have—but she was adorably pretty, which, to most men, is much better.

They both pretended they were very fond of one another, Marjorie because she liked to be kissed and adored, and Gobion because, after bought loves, he found a pleasant freshness. It was not only better and holier, but more piquant. At times, now past, he had persuaded himself that her influence was ennobling and purifying, but the cynicism engendered by evil was burning this feeling out.

He was rapidly getting into the condition when everything loses its savour. Despite his emotional and sympathetic nature, the least glimpse of higher things was going, and though he put the thought from him, he knew in his inmost soul that the time was approaching when life would have nothing more left. Meanwhile it was pleasant to linger in this last gleam of sunshine— to run his fingers through his lady's hair.

He spent the day at the house, meeting old Mrs. Lovering at lunch. She was a lady of the old school, with a black knitted shawl, and the three graces pictured on a cornelian brooch. She disapproved of her granddaughter as too modern, and taking things too much for granted. Indeed, the old lady had a dim idea that Marjorie must be one of the "new" women she had read of in the papers, though if she had ever seen that sexless oddity she would have rescinded her opinion with a gasp of relief.

After a drive in the park, sitting on the front seat of the barouche with Marjorie, and holding her hand under the carriage rug, Gobion went home. The fire had gone out, leaving the room dark and cheerless, in sympathy with his thoughts. But then came a stroll for a few yards in the bright and animated street to the "copy shop," and by the time he got there his spirits had returned.

They were all there, and he soon forgot everything else in the pride of dominating them and making his presence felt.

Sturtevant, who was known in the place, came in, and they had a jolly riotous time, the estimable Mr. Heath having to be sent home in a cab long before closing time.

Sturtevant drank till he was white and shaking, but kept quite sober, and was as caustic as ever. Wild dramatically related, amid shouts of laughter, how he had first met his *protègè* Blanche Huntley, when he was reporting in the divorce court. It was one of his dearest memories. Altogether it was a most successful evening.

Then came a week of terribly arduous work, from nine in the morning till late at night, varied for Gobion by two or three flying visits to the Loverings. Night after night they wrote with the whiskey bottle between them. MS. after MS. was finished and sent off to be typed; and then when they had produced a number of articles, paragraphs, and stories, possibly unequalled in London for their brilliancy and falsity, they both went to bed in Sturtevant's rooms for a day and a half, utterly speechless and worn out.

When the copy was despatched, for Gobion there was a period of peace and Marjorie. And for three or four days, while Sturtevant sat in his rooms and drank, Gobion sunned himself in a cleaner air, while the "copy shop" was deserted.

CHAPTER V.

A PSYCHOLOGICAL MOMENT.

There was once a wood-louse, who, being dissatisfied with his position, called himself a Pterygobranchiate. This arrogation of dignity was much resented by his friends. "You belong to the Bourgeoisie," they said to him, "and we cannot call to mind that you have done anything to warrant an assumption of this aristocratic title." "My good fools," said the wood-louse, "you mistake the term 'Bourgeoisie.' The Bourgeoisie are not a class. A Bourgeois is merely a man who has time to sit down, a chair is not a caste." So saying he took another glass of log-juice, and looked his friends steadily in the face. He was an epigrammatic wood-louse.

They returned somewhat abashed, and for a time, though he was not liked, he was asked about a good deal; for as people said, "To have a Pterygobranchiate in one's rooms lends a party such an air of distinction."

Our friend made some mistakes at first, for he could not resist the dishes of dried wood *á la Française* and the '74 log-juice that were of frequent occurrence at the tables of the great. The result of this was that Nemesis, in the shape of gastric pains, overtook him, and he had to moderate his appetites.

"Indigestion," he said, "is charged by God with the enforcement of morality on the stomach, I will reform my habits." Another reason also contributed to this wise decision, for one day, when going to the kitchen for his boots, he heard the cook (an elderly wood-louse of uncertain temper) say to the boy wood-louse who cleaned the knives and helped in the garden: "Master's that independent and 'e smell so of drink since 'e 's been a Pterygobranchiate, there's no bearin' with 'im." He realized how foolish he must look in the eyes of many good people, so he pitched his new visiting cards into a rabbit-hole, and once more returned to middle-class respectability and happiness.

This story has seven morals, only one of which is wanted here, and that is: "Any divergence from habit is generally attended with disastrous results." This was the case with Gobion, who, in an unguarded moment, told Mr. Lovering something approaching the truth, and so gave himself away.

The three or four days at the close of the Loverings' visit were very enjoyable to him, especially after the hard work of the last week; but unfortunately Mr. Lovering could not quite understand what he was doing in London, and after a time bluntly asked him the reason for this change of plans. Thereupon Gobion admitted that he had had a disagreement with his father, and the parson putting two and two together arrived at a guess that was not far short of the truth.

Both of them were humbugs, but with this difference, that while Gobion knew it and made it pay, Mr. Lovering prayed night and morning that he might not find it out. The result was that the clergyman, who, as the father of a most attractive damsel, naturally desired to sell her to an eligible bidder, took Marjorie home at once, telling her that he had been "greatly deceived" in Gobion, and dictating a polite little note which she sent him.

He got the letter while he was at breakfast, and read it slowly, trying in vain to feel it as a blow. It was of no use, however, for it did not even lessen his hunger for the meal before him.

Then in a flash he realized what this callousness meant. It meant simply this, that the actual moment had arrived when all higher aspirations had deserted him, that he was inevitably and firmly bound to sin, while his mind was allowed to realize the horror of it.

His soul had passed into the twilight.

He knew all this in the space of time that it took to pour out a cup of coffee, but not a muscle of his face moved.

He knew the reaction would be torture when it came—the torture of a man damned before death—but until then there was the hideous joy of absolute unrestraint. There would be no more even shadowy scruples, he would frolic in evil over the corpse of a dead conscience.

He rang the bell for some more bacon and a morning paper. While he was reading a "Drama of the Day" article by Clement Scott, the landlady knocked at the door, and said, "Please, sir, a boy messenger has brought this, and is there any answer?" He took the note.

"Dear Mr. Yardly Gobion,—I and Veda are going to *The Liars* to-night, and we want you to escort us. Come to dinner first if you can.

"Yours, E."

He scribbled an acceptance and sent it back by the boy. The invitation came from a Mrs. Ella Picton, the wife of Lionel Picton, the editor of the well- known paper *The Spy*. Gobion had been to her house several times, and she had petted and made much of him.

Her husband was a clever, sardonic man, who let his pretty wife do exactly as she liked. He said that marriage resembled vaccination, it might take well or ill, and as for him he put up with the result for quietness. To his great amusement, his wife had almost persuaded herself that she was in love with Gobion. He looked so young and fresh, with such a pretty mouth, and such expressive eyes. She felt a desire to taste all this dawn.

Picton quite understood, and resolved to use Gobion for his own purposes, as it seemed necessary to have him in the house. Accordingly after dinner he asked him a good many questions about *The Pilgrim* and its editor. His tongue being loosened by champagne, Gobion made fun of Heath, an easy subject of ridicule, and blasphemed against *The Pilgrim*.

"Heath is a sort of literary fat boy, an urchin Rabelais," he said.

"Look here, I'll give you ten guineas for a column in *The Spy*, showing up Heath and *The Pilgrim*. You needn't give names. Just make it racy, and cut into the old elephant. You'll excuse my talkin' shop in my own house, but I should like to have you on *The Spy* very much."

Gobion was flattered. *The Spy* was disreputable, but big and important. He agreed to do an article for the next issue, and as the arrangement was concluded, the butler came in to say that the ladies were ready to start. Bidding his host good-night, he went up to the drawing-room, where Mrs. Picton and her sister Veda Leuilette were waiting.

They drove to the "Criterion," and the air of the carriage was heavy with the scent of flowers and a subtle odour of white lilac, and the *frou-frou* of skirts seemed to accentuate the perfume. They drove up to the theatre, the footman springing down to open the door, and Gobion helped the ladies out. As they went into the *foyer* he noticed Wild and Blanche Huntley going into the stalls. It was very pleasant to take care of two strikingly pretty women, and Gobion was conscious of a wish that some of his Oxford friends, who had imagined that his flight to London practically meant starvation, could see him now.

The house was full of celebrities. There were warm scents in the air, and from their box they could see vaguely as through a mist a parterre of bright colours, the swirl of a fan, the gleaming of white arms, and the occasional sharp scintillation from a diamond ring or bracelet, while beyond, the space under the circle was crowded with rows of white faces framed in black.

Mrs. Picton was dressed in pale blue *crêpe-de-chine*, looking very lovely, and her violet eyes flashed a dangerous fascination while Gobion and she consulted the programme. Soon after their entrance the band came in, and began to play a lazy, swinging waltz, which seemed to Gobion to harmonize strangely with the apricot light of the theatre. The whole scene struck an unreal and exotic note; he felt a strange deadening of thought, a dreamy sensuousness more physical than mental, and every time Mrs. Picton leant back to make some remark, with a little flash of white teeth framed in wine-red lips, her looks stung his blood.

One of her hands lay on the cushion of the box, white and soft, with rosy filbert nails.

"How Botticelli would have loved to paint your hands," he said, speaking a little thickly.

"A portrait is always so unsatisfactory, don't you think?"

"Perhaps; a looking-glass is a better artist than Herkomer."

"Now you're going to be clever! Look at Mrs. Wrampling in the stalls—fancy showing so soon after the divorce! Isn't she a perfect poem, though?"

"One that has been through several editions."

"She's well made up, but she's put on a little too much colour."

"Oh, she's not as ugly as she's painted."

"Now you are much too nice a boy to be cynical."

"The cynic only sees things as they really are."

She laughed a silvery little laugh. "Who is that ugly man with her?"

"That is *the* man—Wilfrid Fletcher."

"She must be fonder of his purse than of his person."

"The most thorough-going of all the philosophies."

"Who else is here that you know?"

"Well, that very fat man in the third row is Heath, the editor of *The Pilgrim*. He was at Exeter—my college—years ago."

"I should have imagined that he was a University man."

"Really! Why?"

"He is so evidently an apostle of the Extension movement."

"That's quite good! Heath is a clever man though, despite his size."

"In what way?"

"He manages to grasp the changeful modern spirit of the day exactly."

"I think I was introduced to him once, somewhere or other."

"I believe he does go into society."

"Society condones a good deal."

"It is condonation incarnate."

She looked up at him, and blushed a little. "Perhaps it is as well?"

"For some of us?"

"*Si loda l'uomo modesto.*"

"Don't you think modesty is advisable? One never knows how far to go."

"One should experiment, then; modesty is more original than natural nowadays."

"Originality is only a plagiarism from nature."

She opened her fan, moving it quickly. She was not accustomed to be fenced with like this.

Gobion's senses were coming back to him, the voluptuousness had gone, and after the first intoxication of her presence, he looked again and found she did not interest him in the way she sought. After the first act he offered to get them some ices, sending them by a man, while he went to the buffet.

Heath and Wild were there. "Hullo!" said the former, "who's that pretty woman in your box?"

"Picton's wife."

"Lionel Picton?"

"Yes."

"I wouldn't advise you to get mixed up with that lot," he said, making Gobion feel rather guilty as he remembered the article he was going to do for *The Spy*. After a minute Wild moved away.

"Such a joke," said Heath, with a grin. "Wild's brought little Blanche Huntley, the typewriter girl, and both Mrs. Wrampling and Will Fletcher are here, and they're saying that Wrampling himself is in the circle! It's a dirty world, my boy, a dirty world."

"I wouldn't quarrel with my bread and butter if I were you," said Gobion; "you and I'd be in rather a hole if it wasn't for these little episodes. Mrs. Grundy always was an indecent old person. Ta-ta, see you after at the 'copy shop'?"

"Yes, my wife's away in Birmingham, so I won't go home till morning."

Gobion went back to the box, where he found Moro de Minter, the new humourist, making himself agreeable. Gobion knew the man slightly, and hated him. People said his real name was Gluckstein, and he was reported to have been a ticket collector at Euston before he had come out as the apostle of the ridiculous. He was holding forth on his latest book, and he asked Gobion what he thought of the new humourists.

"I have only met two sorts," he answered, "the disgustingly facetious and the facetiously disgusting. Both are equally nasty."

Miss Leuilette was rather nettled; she liked Minter.

"And what do you think of the new critics of *The Pilgrim* type, Mr. Minter?" she asked.

"They squirt venom from the attic into the gutter, and nobody is ever hurt." After which passage of arms he left the box, and the curtain went up on the Inn at Shepperford.

After the play Gobion saw the ladies into their carriage, and Mrs. Picton, as she pressed his hand, whispered him to come to tea the next day.

"I shall be quite alone," she said, with a side look.

Then came the "copy shop" and a noisy supper, at which the latest sultry story of a certain judge's wife was repeated and enjoyed.

It struck Gobion more than ever what a drunken, rakish lot these men were, but still he was very little better, only less coarse in his methods, and it didn't matter.

Lucy, the barmaid, was in great form. Someone had given her a copy of *The Yellow Book*, with its strange ornamentation.

"They do get these books up in a rum way now," she said, pointing to the figures blazoned on the cover.

"You shouldn't find fault with that, my dear," he said. "The fig-leaf was the grandmother of petticoats"; and everyone roared.

"Can anyone recommend me a new religion?" said a fat man who did sporting tips for *The Moon*.

There was a yell at once. "Flintoff wants a new religion." "Theosophist!" "Absintheur!" "Jew!" "Mahomedan!"

"Theosophist?" said the fat man; "no, I think not. Madame Blavatski was too frankly indecent. Absintheur might perhaps suit if it wasn't for Miss Marie Corelli. Jew is quite out of the question; there are two difficulties, pork and another. Mahomedan! well, that isn't bad. As many wives as you like—the religion of the henroost. Yes, I think I'll be a Mahomedan."

"How about drinks?" said Gobion.

"Oh, damn! Yes, I forgot that, I must stick to Christianity after all." He limped to the table to get a match.

"What's the matter with your leg?" said Heath.

"I hurt it last night going home in the fog."

"You should try Elliman's—horse for choice."

"I did, and I stank so of turpentine I was quite ashamed to lie with myself."

"You're not ashamed to lie here," said some feeble punster.

"No, it's my profession. I'm a sporting prophet."

Gobion suddenly remembered that he had heard nothing about the mass of copy that had been sent out some days before.

"Has Mr. Sturtevant been in to-night?" he asked the barmaid.

"No, I haven't seen him for two or three days," she said.

Gobion went quickly out into the Strand and walked to Sturtevant's rooms. The gas flamed on the dingy staircase, making a hissing noise in the silence, and shining on the white paint of the names above the door—Mr. Mordaunt Sturtevant, Mr. Thompson Jones, Mr. Gordon.

The "oak" was open, so Gobion went in, pushing aside the swing door at the end of the little passage.

A strong smell of brandy struck him in the face. He walked in, and looked round the screen by the fire, starting back for a moment with a sick horror of what he saw.

The candles were alight before the looking-glass over the mantelpiece. In front of it stood Sturtevant, with his back to Gobion. His thumbs were in the corners of his mouth, and with his first fingers he was pulling down the loose skin under his eyes, making the most ghastly grimaces at his image in the mirror.

Gobion stood still, petrified, and mechanically pressed the spring of his opera hat, which flew out with a loud pop. Sturtevant wheeled round like a shot, shaking with fear. When he saw who was there he gave a great sob of relief and fell into a chair.

"O God, how you startled me!" he said.

"What on earth's the matter with you?" said Gobion; "you look as if you were dying."

The man was not good to look at. His skin was a uniform tint of discoloured ivory, with red wrinkles round the eyes. His lips were dark purple and swollen, his hands shook.

"I'm so glad you've come; I've had a slight touch of D.T., and if you hadn't come in I should have broken out again to-night."

Gobion calmed him as well as he could, and in about an hour got him into something like ordinary condition.

"And now," he said, "how about our copy?"

"By George, I've forgotten all about it; there are probably a lot of letters in the box."

They got them out. The first one they opened was a collection of personal paragraphs sent in by Gobion, "Declined with thanks." The next was a cheque from the *Resounder* for four guineas, in payment of the "Gambling at Oxford" article. They went on opening one after the other, and at the end found that they had netted twenty-six pounds.

Sturtevant got excited about it, and wanted to have some more brandy, but Gobion managed to get him to bed, and locked the door, putting the key in his pocket. He built up the fire, took Daudet's *Sappho* from a shelf, and passed the night on the sofa alternately reading and dozing.

It took him three or four days to bring Sturtevant round to something like form, most of which he spent in the Temple, occupying himself by writing the attack on Heath for *The Spy*.

It was the cleverest piece of work he had done, and when it was finished it was with all the pride of an artist that he read it to Sturtevant, and sent it to Blanche Huntley to be typed.

Meanwhile he became at times horribly bored and low-spirited, and each new attack accentuated the next, for he would rush into the lowest forms of amusement to find oblivion. In the intervals of coarseness he called on Mrs. Picton.

Such society as was open to him soon began to pall, and he spent more and more time at the "copy shop" or with Sturtevant in the Temple.

These two men, who a few years ago were freshmen at Oxford, sat night after night cursing and blaspheming all that most men hold sacred.

They were colossal in their bitterness.

Sturtevant said once, "Life is a disease; as soon as we are born we begin to die. I shall die soon from D.T., and you'll write a realistic study for *The Pilgrim*. Perhaps my life was ordained for that end." Which, considering the degree the man had taken, and what his mental abilities were, was about the bitterest thing he could have said.

One night Sturtevant went to bed about two, leaving Gobion in the room not much inclined for sleep. After an inspection of the bookcase, he took down a Swinburne, and turned to "Dolores."

"Come down and redeem us from virtue,

Our Lady of Pain,"

he read in the utter stillness of the night.

Then he put the book down and sat staring into the fire, thinking quietly of the literary merit of the poem, while its passion throbbed through and through him—a strange dual action of mind and sense.

Suddenly he looked up and saw a silver streak in the dull sky, the earliest messenger of dawn pressing its sad face against the window.

"I will go abroad," he said, "and see the day come to London." He went out in the ancient echoing courts through the darkness, till he came to the Embankment, and looked over the river. Far away in the east the sky was faintly streaked with grey, the curtain of the dark seemed shaken by the birth-pangs of the morning. He stood quite still, looking towards a great bar of crimson which flashed up from over St. Paul's, showing the purple dome floating in the mist. The western sky over the archbishop's palace was all aglow with a red reflected light. Dark bars of cloud stretched out half over heaven, turning to brightness as the sun rushed on them. The deepening glow spread wider and wider, on and up, till the silver greys and greens faded into blue, and the glory of the morning in a great arch suffused the Abbey, the Tower, and all the palaces of London. The sparrows began to twitter in the little trees on the Embankment.

———————————

CHAPTER VI.

THE COUP.

"He was one of those earnest people who feel that life ought to have some meaning if they could only find it out," said Sturtevant, "and he came in with my little brochure, *The Harmonies of Sin*, in his paw. He was a sort of wrinkled romance. 'Sir,' he said, 'may I ask if you are Mordaunt Sturtevant?' 'At your service,' I answered. Then he said, 'I must tell you that I have felt it my duty to come and remonstrate with you about this 'ere dreadful book.' I asked him to sit down, and pushed over the decanter. He waved it away, tapping my book with his umbrella. 'You have unpaved hell to build your book with,' he said. 'Then my book is made up of good intentions,' I answered, but he didn't see it. 'Think of your pore soul,' he said. I told him I didn't know its address. 'Sir, you have exalted harlotry into a social force.' I told him the harlot was the earthworm of society. He got up and retreated to the door. 'Any *man* would 'ate it,' he said. I asked him quite politely if he considered himself a man. He remarked that he *was* a man, 'made in God's image, sir! in God's image!' 'The mould must have leaked,' I said.

"At this he grew angry, pointing his umbrella at me and snorting. 'You 'ave all the vices, and aspire to all the crimes,' he shouted. When he began to shout I'd had about enough, so I kicked him downstairs."

"When did this episode occur?"

"Oh, just before you came in."

"What's the book about, I haven't read it."

"Merely a little psychological analysis of a young girl's misdoings."

"There's a sort of naked indecency about a young girl's soul, so I don't think I'll read it. Pass the whiskey, will you? You've had enough. I suppose you hurt your visitor considerably?"

"Oh, he didn't really come, I only said that for the sake of saying something, and because I thought how amusing such a man would be if he did turn up."

Gobion yawned. Both of them were very dull and miserable.

The afternoon was all blind with rain swirling against the window in sudden gusts. Footsteps echoed on the flags below with a monotonous clank, while, more faintly, London poured into their ears a dreary hum, a suggestion of wet cold streets. It was about four in the afternoon, and Gobion having done some work in the morning was now in the Temple, sitting in front of the fire, without any present interest. Restless and miserable, he tried to think of Scott, of Father Gray, of the people who cared for him, hoping for vague thrillings, little tender luxuries of regret, but it was of no use. A short time ago he could have induced the pleasing grief-bubble easily with a good fire and a little whiskey, and at its bursting, enjoy a music-hall with its lights and laughter; but now something seemed to have snapped. The curtain was down, the gas was out, the house was cold and empty. He was no longer able to put on a sentimental halo and act at himself as an approving audience.

Sturtevant too was dull and lethargic. He was not emotional like the other, but though a man of less charm, his attainments were greater, he knew more, and now he also was struggling to think—to work.

They were both silent for some time while the darkness closed in, the rain outside pattering with an added weariness and the wind wailing up from the river. At last Sturtevant took up a glass from the table and threw it into the fire with an oath.

"Laugh, you devil!" he said, "shout! be merry! be brilliant!"

"Can't," said Gobion, "I keep my brilliancy for the comparative stranger."

"——and the positive *Pilgrim*, I suppose."

"Exactly. Hallo! there's someone at the door." He shouted, "Yes!" it was one of his little mannerisms never to say, "Come in." The door opened and a girl came round the corner of the screen. It was Blanche Huntley, Wild's mistress, dressed in a long macintosh dripping with rain.

Both men jumped up surprised, Gobion helping her to take off her ulster, while Sturtevant put her umbrella in the stand.

She came to the fireside, a girl not unlike a dainty illustration in a magazine, very neatly got up with a white froth of lace round her neck, and a *chic* black rosette at her waist. Certainly a pretty girl, with a sweet rather tired mouth, well-marked eyebrows, and dark eyes somewhat full, the lids stained with bistre. Gobion knew her, having met her at Wild's, and rather liked her. She was a girl with ideas, and might have made something of her life if she had not been mixed up in the famous Wrampling Divorce Case, and been forced to leave her type-writing office in the City.

When ruin comes a man begs, a woman sells.

She sat down, Gobion introducing her to Sturtevant, who looked with some interest. "Fashion-plate in distress," was his mental comment. Gobion thought, "Her youth is the golden background which shows up the sadness of her lot; lucky man Wild though," a very fair index to the individuality of the two men as far as such things go.

"I'm afraid I've got some bad news for you, old man, and it's partly my fault," she said.

"What is it, Blanche?"

"Well, we were sitting at lunch to-day—Tom wasn't going to the office— when that old pig, Mr. Heath, came rushing in, half mad, waving a paper in his hand, cursing and swearing till I thought they would hear him in the street. He threw it on the table, and I noticed a column in leaded type marked with blue pencil. 'There,' he said to Tom, 'there's a nice thing to see about one's self! Some damn dirty skunk's been writing this about me and *The Pilgrim*.' It was so funny to see him, I never saw anybody in such a bate before; I looked over Tom's shoulder, and, without thinking, said, 'Why, I typed that for Mr. Yardly Gobion.' 'What!' they both yelled. 'Well—I'm—damned! Curse the cad!' Excuse me telling you all this. Well, he went on storming and raving, and said he was going to sack you, and write you a letter you'd remember, and what was more, crab you in every paper in London. I'm horribly sorry, it was all through me."

Sturtevant gave a long whistle.

"Never mind, dear," said Gobion, "it doesn't matter, I don't care; what a rag it must have been!"

"I haven't seen the thing in print yet," said Sturtevant, "I'll go out and get a copy."

When he had gone, Blanche came closer to Gobion. "Poor boy," she said, "I'm afraid you'll find things rather difficult now."

"Never mind, dear, it doesn't matter, I've got past caring for most things. Does Wild know you're here?"

"Tom? oh no, he'd half kill me if he did. He never liked you much, you know, he said you put on such a lot of Oxford side."

"Isn't he kind to you, then?"

"Oh, Lord, no, not now. He was at first, but he's getting tired."

"I should cut the brute."

"What would I do?" she said sadly, "what would I do? I've no character or money or anything. I'd have to go to the Empire promenade, I expect."

She stretched out her hands to the blaze wearily.

"Poor little girl," he said, taking one of her hands in his, "poor little girl, it's a nasty, miserable world."

She said nothing for half a minute, and then she burst into an agony of tears, dropping her head on his shoulder.

"Oh, don't, dear, don't!" said Gobion, half crying too; "try to bear up."

"You don't know what it means. You're not an outcast."

"Yes I am, dear, I'm a good deal worse than you. I have a hell, too. Be a brave girl."

She smiled faintly through her tears.

"You are good," she said, "not like the other men."

"I'm simply a blackguard; don't tell me I'm good."

"You don't shrink from me."

"I? Good God! you don't know what I am—sister."

At that word she crouched down in her chair, passionately sobbing.

"God bless you," she said, "God bless you."

"You must leave him, dear, and get your living by your type-writing." He pulled out his pocket-book and made a rapid calculation. "Twenty here and ten at my rooms. Look here," he said, "I'm not hard up now; here's three fivers. It will keep you going for a month or two. Make a new start, little woman."

She took the money and looked him in the face. Some thoughts are prayers.

"Good-bye," she said, "good-bye. If only I'd met you first."

The man bowed his head, and they left the room hand in hand. When they reached the lane she turned, and in the dim light of the flickering lamp she saw that his face was wet.

He took her little ungloved hand, raising it to his lips, still with bowed head, and turning, left her without a word.

When Sturtevant came in an hour afterwards he found him lying on the floor dead drunk, with a little pool of whiskey dripping from the table on to his hair.

<hr>

"We must do highly moral articles for those papers which are calculated not to bring a blush to the face of the purest girl (except in the advertisements of waterproof rouge), or you might try *The Spy*. They can hardly refuse your copy now," said Sturtevant, about three weeks after the exposure.

Gobion had found the girl spoke truly. Not a paper in London was open to him. He was barred at the "copy shop," and was living on money borrowed from Scott in a piteous appeal full of lies. He forwarded an article to Picton, but it was sent back by return of post, with a sarcastic little note, saying that Mr. Picton could not find himself sufficiently bold to accept any further contributions. Things were getting rather desperate. Oxford bills were coming in by every post to both of them. They were nearly at their wits' end for money.

At this juncture came a letter from Condamine.

"Oxford Union Society.

"Dear Gobion,—The game is played almost to an end. Only one more move, and that not till next June, to be taken. Then will be peace at last. My latest has been of its kind a master-stroke, that is, to disappear. Things were getting too hot for me, so I have gone down to read. Everybody was getting suspicious, and eyed me askance. Drage was sent down (another disappearance!) for lying drunk with a friend from Oriel in the fellows' quad, and for reviling the buck priest most blasphemously in that he had awakened him. My tutor waxed very wroth with me. I was troubled with frightful insomnia every afternoon, and often in the morning—often finding it necessary to go to bed at midnight, rise at two
a.m. and work till five or so, and again retire. Perhaps this was due to the fact that I had to sleep off certain matters of no importance, and then awake early, which is a way of mine. Drage's last moments in Oxford I soothed by fetching Father Gray at ten p.m. Tommy had all sorts of ideas, Stage, Germany, Colonies, every manner of starvation, so I applied his Reverence as a last remedy, which succeeded. Many things I could tell you of this, but not now. He (the Gray father) has got a rich young cub with him, Lord Frederick Staines Calvert, and they are going to town for a time to-day. The boy is without understanding—very oofy
—so if you are still *èpris* with the worthy parson you may be able to make something out of it.

"Farewell. Thine,

"Arthur Condamine.

"To Caradoc Yardly Gobion."

Gobion showed this to Sturtevant. "Do you think there's anything in it?" he said.

"Yes, I certainly do; you must make every effort to get hold of the boy. We must think out a plan; I hope he's an ass. At present he's a problem."

"I'll find him out if I can get hold of him, but I don't quite see how we're going to make any money out of it."

"Do you remember," said Sturtevant slowly, "that dear lady I took to your rooms when I first came up?"

"Little beast! yes."

"I've seen her since then; she lives in Bear Street off Leicester Square, just behind the Alhambra. Now doesn't the diffused white light of your intelligence supply the rest?"

"No, I confess——"

"Listen then. You must tell Father Gray that you are supporting yourself by coaching, and that you are working in the East End. He knows about those defence articles in the *Church Chimes*. Somehow or other he must be got to think you're steady and trustworthy. Then you go about with this young lord he's got and get well hold of him: you can be very charming when you like. From what I have heard of his father, Lord Ringwood, he's been brought up strictly. You must, therefore, take him about a little—Empire, Jimmies, that sort of thing; show him life, till he begins to long to go a little further, and to make sheep's-eyes at the painted ladies in the stalls. Meanwhile I shall get hold of the Bear Street girl and promise her a fiver if she'll help us. One night you and Calvert dine out (give fizz and Benedictine after, it's exciting), and when you get back to your rooms you find Marie as "Mrs. Holmes" waiting to see you. Then I send you a telegram, and you apologise and go out, promising to be back in half an hour. Come round to the Temple, where I shall be waiting. We'll arrange with Marie that she shall have half an hour to make Calvert cuddle her. Then I come in—the outraged husband!—and kick up the devil's own row, swearing I'll get a divorce. In the middle enter Mr. Gobion again. You persuade Marie and me to leave. Then you soothe the ruffled boy, promising to try and arrange the matter. You go out, consult with me, and touch him for a cheque to square matters. I should think we might work a 'thou' almost."

Gobion lay back in his chair, overwhelmed by the brilliancy of the idea. "Wonder-ful! you're a master simply. It ought to be put on the market in one pound shares; and I thought you a mere decadent story writer."

Sturtevant smiled. "Don't say decadent," he said, "it's a misnomer now. The public thinks decadence is the state of being different from Miss Charlotte M. Yonge, while the æsthete——"

"*Please* don't begin to lecture on the utter."

"Do you object to the utter then?"

"I object to the utterer."

"I am silent. The surly word makes the curst squirm."

"That's worthy of Condamine."

Very soon they both got bored again, when the excitement of the plotting had evanesced. It was a consequence of their diseased mental state, this constant overpowering *ennui*. Sturtevant went to the piano and began to chant—

"There was a young fellow of Magdalen
Whose tutor accused him of dagdalen,
    And of stretching his credit;
    He wouldn't have said it
Had the youth been a peer or a lagdalen."

"I hope our lagdalen will be profitable; if we do well we might go down to the Riviera for a week or two."

"That wouldn't be bad at all, the sunny South! I think I'll go west now to the War Office and get Bobby Burness to come out for some lunch. Do you remember him? little Pemmy man. He got a clerkship by interest. Spends his time round the west now looking out for a moneyed female. Jolly berth he's got, just puts his name in the south-east corner of a few papers, and trots off to the park for the rest of the mornin'."

As he went down the Strand he thought over Sturtevant's plan. It was a good deal nearer the wind than he had dared to go before; however, the thing was certain, something had to be done to raise money. He was not a man who could live on thirty shillings a week, for, even though they failed to amuse him, he could not go without the "extras" of life. He did not, for instance, particularly care for Kümmell with his coffee, but it was as much a necessity to him as a clean shirt.

The morality of Sturtevant's scheme did not trouble him in the least; the danger was the thing he thought of. His head bubbled with details and scenic arrangements, rapidly falling into order as he thought. His mind was masterly in its grasp of salient points, in its suggestions of detail. Naturally, as he plotted and studied his part, this orderly marshalling of ideas induced a sense of freedom from danger. With a clearer view of incident came a confusion of outline.

He had just got to Trafalgar Square when he started to feel a hand placed on his shoulder, and looking round saw Father Gray and his victim. In the first shock of surprise he reeled as if struck, and a flash of deadly fear passed over his face, but so instantaneously that it would have been almost impossible for a stranger to have seen it. Though he had recovered this first feeling of terror in a moment, hard as he was, he could never have prevented it. It was the inevitable cowardice of evil, the most horrid kind of fear. Then almost immediately came a great flood of exaltation dominating all other sensation.

"This *is* jolly," said Father Gray, "we were just coming to see you. This is my friend, Lord Frederick Calvert. How are you getting on? Well! Oh, I'm so glad. You did excellent service for us in the *Church Chimes*; that Protestant paper was dreadfully venomous. Now, what do you say to the hotel and lunch?"

"I should like it of all things. Where are you staying?"

"At the Charing Cross, just over the road."

"Right you are. If you will go on I will join you in a moment; I just want to go to the post."

He went to the office at the corner, and sent off a wire to Sturtevant, not being able to resist elevenpence-halfpennyworth of epigram.

<blockquote>"Everything comes to him who can't wait. Keep away from my rooms, have met our worthy friends.—G."</blockquote>

The lunch party was bright and enjoyable. Lord Frederick did not talk much, but Gobion did, and the clergyman treated him most affectionately, paying the greatest attention to his remarks. The young fellow, who was aching to see a little life, and taste some of the joys hitherto forbidden, looked on Gobion as a being from another world, charmed and fascinated by his manner and conversation. He hoped that perhaps he might be able to make him the excuse for a little more freedom.

At the end of the meal a waiter came up with a telegram in his hand, "Rrreverrend Grray, sir?" he said. The clergyman read the flimsy pink paper, his face growing very serious as he did so.

"My dear Lord Frederick," he said, "I am so very sorry. My great friend Stanley, of the C.B.S., is dying up in Scotland and asking for me. I must leave you for a day or two, I fear. Do you mind? Gobion, perhaps, would not mind keeping you company a little."

Both men showed the deepest sympathy, saying that they could manage very well, while both were inwardly rejoicing. There were the elements of farce in the situation.

They got him off late in the afternoon. "God proposes, and man is disposed of," said Gobion as the train left the station. Lord Frederick laughed. "And now, my dear sir," he said, "I place myself entirely in your hands. To speak quite frankly, I've never had such a chance of a rag before, and I want to make the most of it."

"I too should like a rag," said Gobion. "We *will* rag, and take no thought for the morrow beyond staying up to welcome its arrival. We'd better go and dress first; I'll call at the hotel when I'm ready."

When he had put the other down at Charing Cross he went on in the hansom to the "Temple," bursting in on Sturtevant, whom he found with the female conspirator sitting on his knee. "Arrange the coup for to-morrow evening at nine," he said; "I'm off now to take him round the halls."

He rushed out again and dressed as quickly as he could, putting two or three sovereigns in his pocket for emergencies, though he intended his friend should pay all expenses.

They went at first to The Princes, and had, as Gobion told Sturtevant next morning, "a dinner regardless, my dear boy, simply regardless. Never done so well before." Lord Frederick insisted on paying, explaining that as he had asked Gobion to accompany him, all the expenses would be his.

They got on very well together. The nobleman was ingenuous and gentlemanly, and Gobion, who appreciated these things to the full, almost felt compunction at what he proposed to do. They afterwards went to the Alhambra, taking a box, and Gobion pointed out various people as celebrities in literature and art, making himself a charming companion by his clever commentaries on the crowd.

Being extremely young and innocent, Lord Frederick was of course a confirmed cynic, and he enjoyed the malice of Gobion's remarks, especially as he was always unmercifully snubbed at home when he tried to be caustic.

On this particular evening it happened that no one of any note was in the place except Moro de Minter, the comic journalist, but, nothing daunted, Gobion pointed out various obvious bank clerks and actors "resting" as the leading lights of London journalism. The poor boy believed it all; he was very ingenuous; indeed, he laughed twice, once almost loudly, at one of Little Hich's songs!

They parted late, Lord Frederick a little tipsy, swearing eternal friendship, and Gobion promised to take him to a well-known night club in Soho the following evening.

Progress was reported to Sturtevant next morning over breakfast, and he gave Gobion some valuable hints as to detail. As the evening drew on both of them got rather nervous and excited—the coup was so big, and the chances of failure so many.

They discussed the final arrangements with an affected disregard for danger, sprinkling cheap cynicism as a sort of intellectual pepper to disguise the too strong taste of the undertaking.

"Pan is dead," said Sturtevant, filling up the inevitable tumbler. "Long live Pannikin! And now to play your part; the curtain is going up and the critics are in the stalls. Go out and prosper."

They dined this time at the Trocadero, Gobion thinking that the music would help in producing the necessary high spirits in Calvert, and at the close of the meal he proposed an adjournment to his rooms, as it was yet too early for the night club. When they mounted the stairs a light showed from under the door. "Hallo," said Gobion, "there's someone here"; and meeting Mrs. Daily on the landing, she said Mrs. Holmes was waiting to see him.

"You're in luck," he said to his friend; "she's a charming little woman—acts in burlesques, you know."

Mrs. Holmes rose to meet them. With a keen sense of the comic side of the situation, Gobion noticed that Sturtevant had been there, his gloves were left on the table. The room was evidently arranged by a master mind. An inviting lounge shaded by a screen was placed by the red glow of the fire, the lights were carefully shaded so as not to shine too fully on the artificial beauties of the lady's face. The cushions and chairs exhaled an odour of patchouli (Sturtevant had been round with a spray-diffuser half an hour before), and *Nana* lay open on the table at the page where Georges is drying by the kitchen fire.

Indeed, so far had the thing been carried out, Gobion could not help thinking that something was wrong. No. 999, Queer Street was a little too visible, but the champagne had exhilarated Calvert, and he noticed nothing, and became on confidential terms with "Mrs. Holmes" in no time.

Absinthe was produced, the sickly smell irritating Gobion, who was longing to get out of the hot rooms and the *poudre d'amour* atmosphere.

At last the telegram came. He said, "Awf'ly sorry, old man, but I must go out for half an hour; they want me to do a leaderette for to-morrow's *Happy Despatch* on the 'spinning-house' row. I'll be back very shortly."

He went out in a hurry to the Temple, where he found Sturtevant in evening dress, white and haggard, walking up and down the room.

<hr>

They got the cheque, and Sturtevant cashed it before lunch next morning, and at one o'clock they met in Gobion's rooms to divide the spoil. Over the meal —a dainty repast, ordered to celebrate their achievement—they were in the highest spirits. To-morrow they resolved that they would go to Cannes, or perhaps further still.

"We might do Madeira," said Sturtevant. "Think of the heat, the quivering air, the hum of the insects, ah-h!" He took a deep anticipatory breath, and as he did so the door opened and an elderly gentleman came in.

"I don't think I have the pleasure," said Gobion, rising from his chair.

"My name is Ringwood," said the stranger quietly. Gobion flinched as if he had been struck in the face. There was a strained, tense silence, only broken by the gurgling of the champagne in Sturtevant's glass as he raised it to his lips. Then he sneered, "Ah!" his lips curling away from his teeth.

Lord Ringwood struggled desperately to control himself. "Good God! what a damned couple of rascals you are!" he cried.

Gobion laughed a little sickly, pitiable laugh. "Fine day," he said.

The peer got up. "I see now what to do," he said. "I was a fool to come here. I'll have you both in gaol this afternoon."

When he had gone, and they had heard the front door bang, Gobion jumped up and packed a portmanteau.

"Go back to the Temple," he said; "no one knows your address. I'm going to get rooms somewhere in Pimlico—till we can get further away. I'll come to the Temple to-night."

He got into a cab and drove away. As he turned into the Embankment a piano-organ burst out with "The Dandy Coloured Coon," and the tune throbbed in his brain, keeping time to the monotonous beat of the horse's feet on the macadam.

━━━━━━━━━━━━━━━

CHAPTER VII.

THE CONSOLATIONS OF MRS. EBBAGE; WITH SOME ACCOUNT OF THE REV. PETER BELPER.

In the Vauxhall Bridge Road Gobion found a room in a lodging-house kept by a Mrs. Ebbage. In the evening of the same day he went to the Temple, but found Sturtevant's door shut, and he received no answer to his knocks. As he was turning away he saw that something was written on a piece of paper pinned to the door.

"To Y. G.,—Note for you at the 'Grecian' bar.

"M. S."

He went to the bar and got the letter, which ran:—

"Middle Temple.

"Dear Gobion,—I have gone to the southern heat as we proposed, and shall soon be sailing over the siren-haunted Mediterranean. I enclose a ten-pound note in the hope that a period of enforced sobriety may tend to a worthier life for you.

"Even a wise man is sometimes happy, and I should recommend philosophy to you at this present juncture. As a matter of fact, you may be quite sure that Ringwood won't make any move; but still, as I intend, as you know, to practise at the bar, it may be as well to go away for a time.

"If I were you I should stick to journalism; it will pay for bread and butter. You might even write on subjects that you know something about!

"With your appreciation of 'master-strokes' you cannot but admire this my last move. To you, I am sure, the illustrious will now become the august.

"Mordaunt Sturtevant."

"Yes," muttered Gobion, "he is cleverer than I am—ten pounds, out of a thousand! Damn the scoundrel!" He swore under his breath for a minute or two, but his quick wit soon grasped the humour of the situation. Though it told against him, the joke was too good to be lost, and he could not help a somewhat bitter laugh.

He went to bed when he got back, and, having nothing particular to do, lay far into the morning, listening lazily to the sounds of the house. He heard Mrs. Ebbage shouting angrily at her children, while in the distance a tinkling piano spun out "Belle Mahone," and every half-hour or so someone on the other side of the wall knocked his pipe out against the mantelpiece.

A smell of steak and onions floated into the room.

He looked round. It was what is known as a "bed-sitter" on the ground-floor at the end of the main passage. He got up and looked out of the window, making the discovery that the landlady and her family lived below him. Opposite the window, some four yards away, was the straight wall of the next house, while below he looked down into a deep yard into which the back door opened. It was entirely enclosed by the two houses, forming a sort of pit or well. Some children were playing in the dirt, while just below his window a rope was fastened, with some socks and a flannel shirt drying on it.

His room was furnished with the bed, a jug and basin standing on an old sugar-box painted green, an old armchair, a table, a wooden chair, and a mirror over the fire, in which a crack down the middle was repaired by a strip of paper gilded to match the frame. The walls were decorated with a black japanned pipe-rack studded with pink and green stars, a medallion of the Queen stamped in bronze cardboard, and a photograph of the new Scotland Yard framed in shiny yellow wood.

For this he was to pay five-and-sixpence a week. Strangely enough the utter sordidness of the place did not strike a jarring note. He felt that he had dropped out of everything, that from henceforth he belonged to this world of Mrs. Ebbage, this Vauxhall-Bridge-Road world. After another lazy half-hour he got up and dressed, calling for the landlady when he was ready. The woman came in, carrying a tray with his breakfast. She was dirty and unkempt. Her face, where it was not black, was yellow, and stray wisps of grizzled hair blew round it—a face lined and shrewd.

"Thort you'd like an 'errin'," she said. "Ebbage 'ad one before 'e went out. 'E's a pliceman, is Ebbage; 'as 'is beat down Kennington way."

"Oh, thanks very much; very nice," said Gobion, amused to see her making the bed and lighting the fire while he ate.

"Better 'ave the window open," she said. "Gets a bit smelly in the mornin', don't it?" She opened the window, breaking off her conversation to shout at one of the children in the yard. "Leave off playin' with Mr. Belper's socks, little nosey wretch yer; always nosin' about, little devil."

"Ah, you don't know what kids are, you don't. Ebbage gets cussing at them sometimes. I sez to 'im, 'Touch the 'arp lightly, my deah! You want yer ugly 'edd tappin',' I sez. It makes 'im fairly med. 'Cummere,' I sez, 'call *your*self a man? Cummere if you want to knock anyone about. I could make a better yuman man than you, art of a lump o' coal.' Ah, 'e isn't what 'Olmes was, my first man. 'E *was* a man—big, fat, fleshy devil, makin' 'is three quid a week regular. 'E was always good to me; 'e was fond of women. I've 'eard 'im say as a man ort to ave as many women as 'e could keep."

Gobion soon got used to the woman, and even began to like her. She was kind to him in her way, saying she'd "had many a toff down on his luck with her," and she "noo the brand." He made friends with the husband—a big, black-haired man, stolid and obscene in his conversation, and they used to go to the public-house at the corner for a "drop of Scotch." Mr. Ebbage always called it "a drop," though it would have been better for him if he had never exceeded the twopennorth that did duty for the aforesaid generic name.

After a fortnight Gobion settled down to a dull cheerless time, sordid and dreadful; and it was but rarely that a pain-flash disturbed his torpor. He used to play the old cracked piano in the evenings to the family. Mrs. Ebbage's nieces—giggling shop girls—would come in from College Street, and he would sit, with no tie and a dirty shirt, making vulgar love to "Trot" and "Fanny," while Ebbage read the football *Star*, and his wife cooked the sausages for supper. Sometimes in the long dull afternoons Lucy Ebbage, a girl of sixteen, used to come into his room and sit on his knee. He took a diseased pleasure in lowering himself to their level.

He was a man with a keen eye for beauty, a deep appreciation of the poetry of things, and yet for a week or two, with a strange morbid insensibility, he revelled in the manners of the vulgarest class in London. "Human nature is much of a muchness," he said to himself. "Why give myself airs? I should make Lucy a capital husband; we could keep a fried-fish shop and be happy."

This went on for three weeks; then one evening—somewhat of the suddenest —came the reaction.

He was sitting alone on the one comfortable chair drawn up close to the fire. The dancing flames lit up the unmade bed, the remains of a chop, a heap of clothes scattered over a chair, and a pair of muddy boots drying in the fender.

It was again the after-dinner hour—an hour with the monopoly of some effects. He sat lazily smoking a pipe, half dozing, when he became conscious of a banjo playing a comic song: "And her golden hair was hanging down her back." Gradually the air took greater hold of him. The distant twanging seemed fraught with an undercurrent of sadness, a sub-tone of regret.

Gradually the sordid message dispelled lassitude, and his vivid mind began to preen itself, waking from its long sleep. First passed away with the swing of the first line the dull December London. His mind put on wings, flying through confused memories to the first night of term, the little Oxford theatre crammed with men—all the old set, Fleming, Taylor, Robertson, Raymond, Young, "Weggie" Dibb, Scott, even Condamine. How they had applauded and joined in the choruses! how they had cheered the fat principal boy, how bright and *young* it was!... Then a moment's hush, and the sharp-strung chords, when the orchestra dashed madly into the song, "Oh, Flo, 'twas *very* wrong, you know!" How all the men had roared at the girl's conscious wink. From the first he had posed, but in those early terms he had been innocent of great wrong ... and now?... The twang stopped with a little penultimate flourish before the final chord. The trams in the road rattled past. Mrs. Ebbage shouted in the kitchen, opining that her spouse must be "off 'is blooming onion"; and outside in the passage Trot and Lucy giggled, high in the palate, hoping he would hear and ask them to come in.... He shook violently in his chair. To his excited imagination it seemed as if strange lights passed before him; he heard strange sounds. He shook, and it seemed as if the scales fell from his eyes, letting all the horror of his life flash into his ken. There was a sense of the finality of things; he saw dimly a far-off purpose.

It was the *staleness*, the torture of sin, not a sorrowful sense of evil, that settled round him like a cloud. He had fed his appetites too heavily, and a total apoplexy of mind and soul had ensued.

Then came a knock at the door, and a grotesque figure entered—a large, gross old man, with heavy pouches under the eyes, with unsteady dribbling lips, dressed in a long parti-coloured dressing-gown.

He said he lived on the other side of the passage, "and perhaps his young friend would come in and smoke a pipe with him." They went into a room much the same as Gobion's. A jug of steaming water stood on the table by a bottle of gin.

"My name is Belper," said the old gentleman, "the Reverend Peter Belper, though I no longer have a cure of souls. Will you have some Old Tom? I never work, but it makes me very thirsty."

Gobion drank; he was not in a state of mind to be surprised at anything. This leering old satyr seemed quite natural and in proper sequence.

"I won't ask you what you've done," he said to Gobion. "A gentleman doesn't live here for no reason." He spoke with a wagging of his heavy jaw, with a hoarse bleat, but an accent in which still lingered a trace of culture.

"No," said Gobion; "I suppose we're a shady lot in this hole."

"We are, we are; I myself am not what I was. Good heavens! I was once a vicar! I am now a moral object-lesson. I used to live by sermonizing, now I sermonize by living. A university man, may I ask?"

"Yes—Oxford."

"Really, there are then two of us. Mrs. Ebbage ought to congratulate herself."

"Have you been with her long?"

"Six years now. I have a moderate incompetence left; enough to be constantly drunk on."

"You find it really does deaden thought?"

"My dear sir, if it wasn't for gin I should long since have been in another hell!"

A shrill laugh floated up from the kitchen.

"I call her 'laughing water,'" said Mr. Belper.

"You are poetic."

"Yes, my father was Belper the minor poet. I am the least poetic of his works."

He leered at the fire, shaking with drink—a shameless, dirty old man. "I was a pretty fellow in my time," he said, licking the chops of remotest memory. "I had a conscience, and wrote harvest festival hymns with it."

Gobion filled his glass. "What do you do with yourself all day?"

"Drink and sleep, sleep and drink."

"Cheerful!"

"Yes, very; what else can I do? My mind is gone; if I think it's only blurred pain. I used to try and philosophise, but I can't think now. I don't believe in the nonsense people talk about the comforting powers of philosophy."

"Nor I. Philosophy seems to me to be an attempt to eat one's own soul, and indigestion generally results."

The old man filled his pipe anew, his face half in light half in shadow, the gross imprint of vice showing more sharply for the contrast, and suggesting still worse possibilities. Bad as it was, it had the prepotency of lower depths.

They often sat together thus, spending the long-drawn evenings over the gin-bottle, japing at society. Mr. Belper was ribald and cynical. Nothing could shock either of them; their only prejudice was to persuade themselves that they had none.

It was a dark, dull time, too sordid for the actors to accrue any excitement at its lurid aspects. Night after night they sat till they were too befuddled to talk, each in turn providing the necessary amount of gin for the night's debauch. Belper punctuated the weary days by long sleeps, and Gobion by caressing Lucy Ebbage.

His health began to go slowly, and the torture of insomnia was added to his life.

One evening Mrs. Ebbage came into his room incoherently reminiscent, and sitting on the bed, rambled of the past, giving Gobion a strange glimpse of the habits of her class.

She told of her youth in a Westminster slum, of her mother who had been kicked to death in a low public-house on the evening of the Derby. "'Er face was like a bit of liver after they'd done with 'er, and when the p'lice came in she was as dead as meat. I often think ovver."

She went on to talk of her daughter by her first marriage, who had died at seventeen, her coarse voice trembling as she told how clever she had been at crochet work, and what a small foot she had. She showed Gobion a tiny white shoe the girl had worn. It was piteous to hear her—this scraggy, hard woman —with tears in her eyes, talking of her dead darling.

Then she said, "My 'ands are all mucky, and I've gone and soiled the shoe. Pore 'Arriet, it don't matter to 'er now."

She wiped her eyes with the corner of her apron, and with a change of manner —a somewhat futile arrogation of gaiety—"We're goin' to 'ave a bit of supper. Ebbage said as 'e could swallow a Welsh rarebit and a drop of something 'ot; come down and 'ave a bit."

"Yes," said Gobion slowly, "let us eat, drink, and be merry, for to-morrow ——"

Mr. Belper came in and made coarse jokes, to Mr. Ebbage's huge delight. Gobion in his loneliness sat and became one of them, eating with his knife to avoid the appearance of eccentricity.

About eleven o'clock he went out with a jug to get some beer. The streets were heavy with fog, but he had not far to go, as the public-house he frequented was just round the corner. He chatted with the barmaid while she was drawing the beer, noticing with a smile the notice painted on the wall:

"Where else can you get

Such fine Mellow 4d. Rum!
Such pure Old 6d. Whiskey!

Such luscious   4-1/2d. GIN!
Such MATCHLESS   6d.   BRANDY!"

As he was going back a man in evening dress knocked against him.

"I beg pardon," he said. "I don't see—good God! Gobion!"

It was Scott.

Gobion took him into his room, and lit the little alabaster lamp, rich in gaudy flower work. The door opened, and the Reverend Peter Belper came in. The light shone on him, and he looked more Silenus-like than ever. "Beg pardon," he said, "thought you were alone." Gobion seized the momentary diversion of his coming to put on a tie and push his dirty cuffs under the sleeves of his coat.

"Oh! my dear old man," said Scott, looking round the room, "have you come to this? Why didn't you tell me?"

He put his arm on his shoulder, and Gobion drew nearer, shaking with emotion.

"I've been always thinking of you," said Scott. "It's been so lonely without you—so dull and lonely—we all miss you so. They said at Oxford that you'd been mixed up in some beastly newspaper scandal, but I knew of course that you'd rather die than do anything like that. I've been horribly afraid for you. You see, I couldn't find out where you'd got to or anything. You look terribly ill, old man; you must come out of this hole. Come away with me to-morrow, and when you're better you can make a new start."

"It's no use," said Gobion, "I'm finished—mind and body."

"Rot, old man! you're only rather pippy. Don't you know you've *always* got me? Don't you remember how once for a joke in those Ship Street rooms you made me put my hands between yours and swear to be your man? Well, it wasn't a joke—to me. Don't you know how we all love you? Fancy your being here, you who used to lead us all. Damn it all, what gaudy nonsense I'm talking!"

His rather commonplace face shone strangely. He seemed to change the mean aspect of the room, to annihilate its sordidness.

Late at night Scott went back to his hotel, promising to be round first thing in the morning to take Gobion away. They parted at the door with a long hand-grip, and never met again in this world.

When he had gone Gobion went back to his room and fell like a log on to the floor, lying there motionless till the grey light crept into the court.

Then he got up and swiftly packed a small bag, his face white and drawn.

He went into the next room. The lamp was still burning, and old Mr. Belper lay in a drunken sleep on the bed. His mouth was open, and he breathed heavily.

Gobion woke him. "I've come to say good-bye," he said.

"What! has it come to that?"

"Yes."

The old man stared heavily. "Well, good-bye," he said. "I shan't be very long either. I'm glad we've met. I, ahem, I—er"—he coughed—"I congratulate you." He passed his dirty hand over his eyes. "Yes, I—er—congratulate you. I wish—I'll see you out."

He came to the front door. They shook hands. "Good-bye," he said, "good-bye, dear boy."

He stood on the steps, a fat, grotesque figure, and watched Gobion's slim form disappear in the fog—a dirty, shameless old man.

CHAPTER VIII.

THE FINAL POSE.

He felt that the time had come at last. What in his misery he had thought vaguely possible now loomed close before.

With the resolve to make an end of it all, to have done with pain, to cheat the inevitable, came a flood of relief. The torture of his brain was swept away as if it had not been, and its receding tide left only a shallow residuum of false sentiment.

The poor fool busied himself with details and accessories. Since he had come to the point, he resolved that he would pose to the last. He began to play his old trick of exciting a diseased duality of consciousness.

As he walked eastwards he was composing his farewell letters, he was picturing to himself the sorrow of his friends. They would talk of him wonderingly, as a brilliant life promising great things, gone with its work undone. They would recall his sweetness, the glow of his bright youth ... the tears came into his eyes at the idea, it was so pathetic a picture.

His thoughts had run so long in the same groove, that though he felt dimly that there ought to be other and deeper feelings within him, he was unable to evoke them. He was conscious that this dainty picturing was utterly false; yet, try as he would, he could not stop it. Whether it was the last flicker of intense vanity, or merely that his mind was weakened by debauchery, it is impossible to say; but when a man plays unhealthy tricks with his mind, and is for ever feeling his spiritual muscles, the habit holds him fast as in a vice. His last hours possess a strange psychological interest.

He walked eastwards mechanically, but stopped when he had turned into Houndsditch, and the roar of the early traffic in Bishopsgate sounded less loudly.

From a card hanging in a pawnbroker's window he saw a bedroom was to let, and after paying the rent in advance, he was allowed to take possession. He lit the oil-stove that did duty for a fire, and lay down, falling into a heavy, dreamless sleep.

When he woke it was quite dark, and after washing his hands he went to a low eating-house for a last meal. The *menu* was pasted on the window in strips, while a cabbage-laden steam floated out of the half-open door. The room was long and low of ceiling, each table standing in a separate partition. A large woman, dressed in a scarlet silk blouse, walked up and down the centre gangway, taking the orders, which she shouted out in a hoarse voice to the open kitchen at the far end. "Pudding and peas!" "Roast, Yorkshire, and baked!"

The table at which Gobion sat was covered with oil-cloth, and as he moved a saucer full of salt out of the way of his elbow, a many-legged insect ran over it to a crack in the wall.

The woman brought him the food, not giving him a knife and fork till he had paid for what he had ordered. He noticed her hands were red and misshapen, with long, black nails.

He ate ravenously. Over the low partition he could see a Jew jerking some rich, steaming mess into his mouth with a curious twist of the wrist, and every now and again wiping his mouth on the sleeve of his coat. These details fascinated him.

When he had done, he asked for some paper, and with the roar of Whitechapel surging outside he began to write to Scott.

"MY DEAR, DEAR OLD MAN,

Forgive me for what I am going to do. Life seems to me——"

After writing a sentence or two he tore it up, as he found that he could not produce what he wanted. Time after time he tried, and only succeeded in being commonplace to the last degree. All his ideas of a tender farewell, a beautiful poetic letter, seemed impossible of realization; instead, he produced effusions which looked as if they might have been copied from the *Family Herald*.

At last he wrote simply "Good-bye," adding his new address. He tried to think of someone else to write to, but could not. His father he hated and feared; there was no thrill in a letter to him. It all seemed very flat and commonplace. These last few hours were not at all as he had pictured to himself.

Then he went out into the Whitechapel High Street. The costermongers' stalls, lit with flaring naphtha lamps, made the street nearly as bright as in the day-time. The pavement was greasy to walk on, and it was thronged by a vast crowd walking slowly up and down. The fog was settling over the houses, and the place smelt like a stale sponge.

He wandered slowly down towards the church, picking his way among the mob.

Coarse Jewish women with false hair shouted to one another. Girls with high cheek-bones, smeared with red and white, caught hold of his arm, whispering evil suggestions to him, and cursing him for a fool when he turned away. There was a lurid glow in the air.

He stopped outside a stationer's window, gazing idly at the specimens of invitation cards in the window.

"Mr. and Mrs. Levenstein

"Request the pleasure of your company

"At the occasion of their son's circumcision."

In the brilliant light he saw the gutters littered with decayed vegetables, bones, and rags. Two old women stood at a corner of the Commercial Road. He heard one of them say, "Yes, it was still-born, so she *said*; but I 'eard it squeak before Annie come out of the room." He passed on. A piano-organ, with a cage of bedraggled birds on the top, struck up, the handle being turned by a boy, while his father went among the crowd showing a smooth white stump where his hand should have been.

The door of the Free Library stood open. He went in. The room was crowded with men standing about reading the evening papers. He walked up and down through the rows of stands, as if looking for someone, after a while coming out again into the street. A sailor knocked against him, and swore at him for a "bleeding fool."

He was passing a pillar-box, when he remembered his letter to Scott, and he posted it, hearing the hollow echo of its fall with the sense of a curious subjective disturbance in the air around. He felt something was by him in the noisy street, something waiting by him for the end. He looked hastily over his shoulder, and then laughed grimly.

After a time, when he had been among the crowd for nearly two hours, some impulse seemed to draw him away, and he went back towards Houndsditch. Before turning down the long narrow street, he went into the "Three Nuns," the big hotel at the corner, and spent his last shilling in three glasses of brandy.

As he closed the door of his lodgings, the noise of the streets sank suddenly into a distant hum, through which he could distinguish the far-off tinklings of the barrel-organ, which had moved higher up the street. When he got to his room he busied himself in making it clean and tidy, clearing up the hearth, putting his clothes neatly away into his bag.

Then he took a little bottle out of his pocket marked "Chloroform." Over the head of the bed he fixed up a sort of rack with two hatpins and some string, so that the bottle could swing exactly over his pillow. Then he pricked a hole in the cork in such a manner that if the phial was turned upside-down, every few minutes a drop of liquid would ooze through.

<hr>

He lit a cigarette and sat down to think. He was not quite sober, but he felt a dull conviction that things were never more unsatisfactory. He felt no sadness, no pathos, stealing over him.

With a great effort he struggled to realize things, getting up and walking round the room, talking thickly to himself. "Here I am, young, clever, of a good family, a man who might have been good or even great; am I going to die like a rat in a hole? Oh, God!" He said it with all the force and yearning he could put into his voice, trying to force a note of pain, but the result was most ordinary. He looked at his face in a little strip of looking-glass above the fireplace. He saw nothing but the imprint of impurity and sin.

Then he lay back on the bed, and thought that he roared with laughter. The situation seemed irresistibly comic. He only chuckled feebly, but to him it seemed as if he were shrieking in an ecstasy of mirth.

Suddenly he got up and fell on his knees, praying aloud, "Oh, God, help me! God forgive me!" All the time that he knelt and tried to pour out an impassioned prayer for forgiveness he knew that it was only an attempt to bring some poetry, some pathos, into his last moments. Again he got up and laughed wildly. His face grew ashen grey and horribly drawn in his attempts to deceive himself, to pose once more.

"Is there nothing, NOTHING? Good God!... why can't I feel? Why? why? Ah! ahh!" He tore at the bed-quilt wildly, snarling like a beast.

<hr>

In the middle of his paroxysm he stopped suddenly and stiffened. Once more the weird horror of another presence in the room came over him. He whimpered like a dog, shrinking into a corner, with staring eyes, not knowing what he did, muttering "Mother—mother!" Then with a complete change of tone and manner, he said, "A nonentity with most seductive hair."

He took the little bottle from the table, and hung it mouth downwards in the sling.

He took off his coat and waistcoat, mechanically winding up his watch and placing it on the mantel.

"This is not at all what I had hoped. It is *most* unsatisfactory, quite commonplace, in fact," he said as he lay down on the bed.

He felt a little splash on his cheek, and moved his face out of the direct course of the liquid, which now began to fall more rapidly.

CHAPTER IX.

TWENTY YEARS AFTER. AN EPILOGUE IN TWO PICTURES.

THE FIRST PICTURE.

The Art of Religion.

The church was very full. It was the vigil of All Saints, and Father Scott was to preach.

Far away, the culminating point of the long vista of shadowy arches, stood the High Altar, blazing with lights. The choir had just taken their stalls, and every head was bent low.

An orchestra was reinforcing the organ, and the long silver trumpets, loved of old Purcell, shouted jubilantly, echoing away down the dim clerestory.

Father Scott felt a strange thrill, an uplifting of the heart, at the melody. He stood up in his stall with the rest, a man whose face still showed a trend to the commonplace, but sweetened, almost refined away by something else.

The little sisters of St. Cecily, sweet souls with whom he worked, said among themselves that he had had a dear friend once whom he had loved, and for whom he still mourned and prayed, and that it was this that made him such an eminently lovable man.

Indeed, Sister Eliza had even read a novel he had written in his early days, a mystic romance of a glorious youth who had never come to prime.

The music of the stately anthem swelled up in a burst of praise, the trumpets singing high over all with keen vibratory notes that told of an inner mystery to ears initiate. Then, when Father Gray, an old priest whose days were nearly done, read the lesson, Scott leant back with crossed hands, thinking of old times, of his youth. It seemed to him on this great night of the Church that other and less earthly forms and voices thronged the building. In the Creed, the words "communion of saints" touched him strangely, as they always did; but to-night they came home to him with a deeper meaning.

"God is so good," he thought simply. "Surely He has pardoned him for that one sin. He was so pure and beautiful—very pleasant hast thou been to me." His thoughts wandered disconnectedly, recalling sentences that had struck him, old scenes and scraps of verse. The smell of the incense brought back Cowley or the Sunday evening services at St. Barnabas. He rejoiced in his heart at the stateliness and circumstance of worship around him, and he recalled some old articles in the *Church Chimes*, defending eloquently the "true ritual of holy Church." He had thought them so good, he remembered, such a dignified answer to the other side.

The prayers began, each with its deep harmonized "Amen," which seemed to him in his excited mind long-drawn gasps of thankfulness and worship. He bent his head low in his hands, and prayed humbly for the Church's welfare, and then, with an uplifting of his heart and a great passionate yearning, for his dead friend. He felt very near to him on this feast of the departed.

The time came for him to speak to the long rows of faces. He mounted to the high pulpit in the sweep of the chancel arch, and looked down on the congregation.

He began quietly enough, but gathered power and sonance as his feelings swayed him, drawing for them a picture, an ideal, to which they might all attain, telling them of the sweetness that comes with goodness. He thought of the friend of his youth, and drew an exalted picture of him, while the people sat breathless at the beauty of his words.

Then he said in a hushed voice how he had thought, and liked to think, that round them to-night were the dear ones who had died, that they were watching over them and praying with them that holy night.

Everyone felt the spell of the hour and the voice of the priest, it was most unearthly, dramatic, and effective. Sister Eliza wiped her eyes and thought of the novel, and only poor old Father Gray, worthy man, was fast asleep in the chancel, tired by the long ceremonial day.

Then came the great procession round the church, with its acolytes and crosses, Father Scott walking last in flowered cope. They sang, "For all the saints who from their labours rest," waking a responsive echo in every heart.

Last, and most impressive of all, the long spell of silent prayer, broken at last by the crashing music, and the shuffling feet of the congregation as they left the building. Sister Eliza, as she went out into the cutting night wind, could not help thinking of the novel. It was not a bad novel, but this is the true account.

THE SECOND PICTURE.

A dinner in honour of the law.

"Well, my dear, and who have you got?" said the duchess.

"First of all there's Mr. Mordaunt Sturtevant, the new Q.C., *quite* a nice person."

"He is," said the duchess, "I've met him. Such eyes! Eliza Facinorious said that he made her 'feel quite funny when he looked at her.' You know the sort of person—makes you feel b-r-r-r-r! like that."

"I know," said the hostess. "Then Marjorie Burness is coming—such a dear! knows all the latest stories about everyone."

"I don't think I've met her," said the duchess, "is she quite?"

"Not exactly; she was a Miss Lovibond—Lovering—some name like that. Parson's daughter, Kensington people, dontcherknow; but so amusin'—fat, too, she is."

"Oh!" said the duchess.

"Then there's a Mr. Sanderson Tom asked. He keeps a school board, or wants the poor to live noble lives in Hackney—somethin' of that sort. Eliza Facinorious and the Baron, Lady Darwin Swift, Mr. Justice Coll, Bradley Bere, the new writin' boy, Lord Saul Horridge, and of course the girls. That's all, I think."

"Oh!" said the duchess again.

She was rather a damaged duchess, and very impertinent, but Mrs. Chitters was exceedingly glad to get her. She really *was* a duchess, which, if a woman has no brains, money, or comeliness, is the best thing she can be. She was staying for a week with Colonel Chitters and his wife.

The dinner was for the joy of Mr. Mordaunt Sturtevant, who had just taken silk. The most eminent member of the criminal bar, he would have been Queen's Counsel long ago if it had not been for some vague rumours of his early life.

A footman opened the door, the duchess her eye-glasses, and Mrs. Chitters the conversation. Mr. Bradley Bere was announced, a youth apparently of seventeen, but of a great name; the rich uncleanness of his life almost rivalling his stories, and both being given undue prominence by his friends on the weekly press. Then came Lord Saul Horridge, a tall melancholy man, whose life was crushed by an energetic mother, whose forte was teetotalism, and whose weakness was omniscience.

Mr. and Mrs. Robert Burness came in, were effusively greeted by the hostess, and passed on to amuse the duchess. Mrs. Burness, *nèe* Marjorie Lovering, had grown too stout for flirtation, and feeling the want of a *mètier*, had turned her thoughts to scandal, and achieved a great success. Her husband, a clerk in the War Office, used to say that his wife had a higher regard for truth than anyone he knew—she used it so economically.

Mordaunt Sturtevant and Mr. Justice Coll came in arm in arm, and soon after they went down to dinner.

Sturtevant had grown two small whiskers, and his keen eyes, shaded by bushy brows, made the duchess want to say "B-r-r-r-r!" several times during the evening.

The Baroness Facinorious, an ample and various lady, was taken down by Mr. Sanderson, the education person from Hackney, and they discussed the latest thing in Chelsea churches.

Bradley Bere told Miss Chitters that poetry was the pursuit of the unattainable by the unbearable, hoping she would repeat it as having come from him.

Mr. Justice Coll alone was silent, his whole mind, no large part of him, being given up to the business in hand.

When the gentlemen came up to the drawing-room Sturtevant sat down by Mrs. Burness, and they discussed their host and hostess, both of them telling Mrs. Chitters what the other had said later on in the evening.

When they got tired of scandal Mrs. Burness mentioned that her son had just gone up to Oxford. "To Exeter, you know. Robert says it's an excellent college. We went up for the 'Torgids,' I think they call them—boatin' races, you know—and we had lunch in Bernard's rooms. *Such* nice rooms, all panelled in oak, and only next door to the Hall, which must be *so* convenient in wet weather, don't you think?"

"Have they a high-barred window in the corner looking out into B. N. C. Lane?" said Sturtevant.

"Yes! do you know them?"

"I think so. I believe I used to know a man who had them years ago. He's dead now."

"Oh, *how* romantic! I must tell Bernard! Perhaps his ghost haunts them! *Do* tell me his name."

"A rather uncommon name—Yardly Gobion."

Mrs. Burness grew pale.

"I knew him when I was a girl," she said faintly.

The man gripped a little ornamental knob on the arm of the chair. The people who were coming after the dinner were being announced. He heard Sir Lionel and Lady Picton's names shouted from the door. It was a curious evening.

"Were you a Miss Lovering before you married?" he asked.

“Yes.”

“Then you’re Marjorie!”

“Yes,” she said with a little smile, “I was Marjorie.”

They were silent for a time, and their faces changed a little.

“Rather a fool, wasn’t he?” Sturtevant forced himself to say at last.

“Oh, yes, we flirted a little, don’t you know, but I always thought him rather poor fun.”

“Yes, he wasn’t much. I remember when I was reading for the Bar I did him a service, for which he was not in the least grateful.”

“Yes, he was quite that sort of person.”

“But still,” said Sturtevant, “he was a man possessed of considerable personal charm.”

FINIS.

PLYMOUTH

WILLIAM BRENDON AND SON

PRINTERS